TRAIL
TO
NEW ORLEANS

JIM EDD WARNER

Cover designer: GetCovers
Graphic designer: Deborah Stocco

For the Rampy family, who I have been a part of for over seventy years. My mother's maiden name was Rampy and I have used all of her siblings' names in this book.

TABLE OF CONTENTS

PROLOGUE

My name is Bill Rampy. I have three brothers and four sisters. We were raised in East Alabama. Two of the brothers still live there and are farmers. All four of the sisters are married to farmers close to our home territory. My oldest brother, Troy, lives in New Orleans where he has a store selling dry goods.

Troy and I are the adventurers of the family. The rest of them had no desire to leave Alabama, so far as I knew. Troy and I had no desire to stay.

Troy went to the East Coast of the U.S. and worked on several sailing ships before he settled in New Orleans. There he started a store furnishing needed merchandise to locals and travelers.

Later I left home for an adventure of my own. First, I traveled to New Orleans to see Troy and to work for him for a few months. While I was there, we decided that Santa Fe, in the Spanish territory of Mexico, looked like a good area in which to sell dry-goods. That is especially once Mexico won its independence from Spain and became an independent country. Mexico's independence was looking very likely from news we had been hearing in the summer of 1820.

5

I didn't waste any time heading to Santa Fe. Once we decided I should go, Troy and I got busy planning the trip. It was obvious that starting soon was important. Santa Fe was in the Sangre de Cristo mountains, so I knew I wanted to get there early enough to beat any heavy snows. We were already in the middle of summer, so the sooner I left the better my chances would be for beating early winter weather.

We got together all the maps and other information that could be found to aid me on the trip. It looked like the Red River would be my best route for most of the trip. At some point, it was clear that the river would run out. I would go the rest of the way by the aid of my pocket compass.

I knew the trip from New Orleans to Santa Fe was going to be long; but it would probably be exciting too. Once we had the trip planned, I packed some provisions and loaded them onto two packhorses along with trade goods furnished by Troy. The trade goods consisted of small items such as watches, hand tools, knives and pistols. I also took a few good rifles.

My own rifles were both Hawken made and I liked them a great deal. They were made by the Hawken Brothers in St. Louis and were the best you could buy. The other rifles I took were not Hawken made and I didn't know anything about who made them; but they were dependable and shot straight. That was what mattered most to me in any kind of weapon. When you were out in the wilderness by yourself, you needed equipment you could count on for self-defense and hunting food. In fact, everything you took with you had a role to play and needed to play it well. Whether it was a saddle and bridle or a pocket compass and bedroll, each item was important.

I saddled my horse Morgan, got the pack horses hitched to him and we were off to Santa Fe. It was going to be quite a journey going from New Orleans to Santa Fe. But it was going to be exciting too. I was going to be traveling through country that few Americans had ever experienced.

I took a ferry across the Mississippi River with my three horses, supplies and trade goods. The Mississippi was amazing. I had never seen so much water in my life.

I rode west from the Mississippi to the Atchafalaya River. From there I went north along the Atchafalaya to the Red River. I followed the Red River west for many weeks until it eventually became a stream and then a trickle and then nothing.

That leg of the trip appeared to be about eight hundred miles. It might have been farther. It was difficult to keep track of distance since I didn't have a good map. I mostly just guessed at how far I was going from day to day, depending on trips I had taken before. I was usually pretty good at this type of guessing.

Along the Red River I ran into two different groups of Indians, so my attempts to avoid them did not always work. I was ambushed once and lost both of my pack horses and much of my gear and trade goods. Eight days later, I ran into a hunting party that chased me out of their territory. Luckily, my horse Morgan was fast enough to outrun their ponies or I might not have made it out of there alive.

For the rest of the trip I tried to keep away from the river and travel slow enough to not kick up any large dust clouds that would signal my presence. Traveling slowly did make my trip last longer; but it was successful in helping me avoid contact with any more Indians. I saw Indians often; but from a distance.

At the end of the Red River, I continued across country to the Pecos River. I followed the Pecos for a while until it took me near the Sangre de Cristo Mountains. I headed west into the mountains and finally found Santa Fe. It was a trip I will never forget and one that brought me more than I ever expected.

In Santa Fe I met two people that guided me to Juan Leos, who was a friend of my brother Troy. Juan and Troy had sailed together for a while and become great friends.

Juan had also gone into trading after he returned home to Santa Fe. He owned a trading post between Santa Fe and Taos.

After Juan and I met, we quickly became friends and he invited me to spend some time working with him. I did and we had a good time together.

In mid-December Juan and I joined a group of other Santa Fe area merchants to go to Chihuahua for their annual trade fair.

The route to Chihuahua was well developed and had hosted thousands of travelers over the last couple of centuries. Many immigrants from Spain had settled in Chihuahua. Later some of those immigrants and their families had move on to Santa Fe to help settle that area. Over the years, there had been a great deal of travel back and forth on the road between the two towns.

Unfortunately, the route was mainly wilderness with only a few towns or villages along the way. Just like all wilderness, it was safe as long as nothing bad happened. There was not much in the way of protection except the occasional group of Spanish soldiers. And now that there was a war going on between Mexico and Spain for Mexico's independence, there were few if any soldiers in this part of the country. If a group was attacked by bandits or Indians, they had to defend themselves as best they could.

Our intention had been to take enough men to defend ourselves against anybody that meant us harm. We had a group of men that we thought was big enough, but when another group of men asked to go with us, we accepted their proposal gladly. All of us had been hearing rumors about possible danger along the route that year. So, the two groups went as one caravan.

In spite of our relatively large number of men and other preparations we had made, there was one Indian attack that cost us the lives of two of the men with us. I was also seriously injured; but survived thanks to Carlos in our group. He had been trained in medical procedures when he was in the Spanish Army. Carlos took good care of me, and for that, I will always be grateful.

Our trip to Chihuahua took about 25 days. The trip was between five and six hundred miles, so it was not an easy ride.

I had been laying in the bed of wagon driven by Juan for much of the trip after the Indian attack. Thanks to Carlos' skill I got better fairly quickly considering my injury. It was a tough couple of weeks until I was well enough to ride upright in the wagon or on my horse Morgan. By the time we finally got to Chihuahua, I was feeling a great deal better. It was exciting to get to the city I had been thinking about for two months.

Many of the men in our caravan, including Juan, had friends and relatives in Chihuahua. At a fiesta style meal in the city center the evening we arrived in Chihuahua, most of the men were able to get together with their families and friends for the meal and a dance. I didn't dance; but the music was exciting.

Juan introduced me to his Aunt Anita and Uncle Claudio and their three grown children: Frances, Josepha and Ronaldo. Ronaldo, who was the oldest, was studying at the cathedral to be a priest. Josepha had just finished school in Chihuahua and was trying to decide what to do next.

Frances was the middle child. She had just returned from Mexico City where she had been studying for several years to be a teacher. She was going to be a teacher at the primary school in the cathedral. Frances and I spent quite a bit of time together over the next three weeks and fell in love. She is the reason for my heartache now. She is lovely and intelligent and special in too many ways to name.

I certainly didn't want to leave Chihuahua and Frances, though I was obligated to go back to New Orleans to tell my brother Troy what I had learned about trading in Mexico. I told Frances that I loved her and wanted to make a life with her. I told her I would return as soon as I could. She told me that she loved me and would wait for my return. But still, I could barely stand being apart from her.

1 | RETURN TO SANTA FE

After twenty-two days on the trail coming from Chihuahua, I was excited to get to the outskirts of Santa Fe. The town looked warm even though we were still in late February, 1821. Chimneys at homes along the road looked like they were welcoming us, as the smoke curled up to the sky.

Every man in our caravan was returning home to Santa Fe after attending the annual trade fair in Chihuahua. They were all businessmen in Santa Fe or the surrounding area.

I was glad to get to Santa Fe, even though I still felt lonely having left Frances in Chihuahua. Frances was going to stay with her family in Chihuahua while I would go on to Missouri, and eventually to New Orleans to tell my brother Troy about my trip.

I promised Troy I would report back to him about trading opportunities I found in Santa Fe and Chihuahua. After that I was going to return to Frances as fast as I could, so we could marry and make a life together.

Returning to Santa Fe was one step toward getting back to Frances, so I was glad to be there. It was a comfortable and friendly town. I was glad to get back; but I didn't intend to stay long.

Our caravan continued until we got to the town square where we had started from over two months before. We stopped in front of the cathedral where a crowd of family members had come to welcome us back and talk about our trip.

Juan's mother and father were there. They had already heard of my relationship with Frances. They were pleased and hopeful that I would hurry back. Juan's family had already accepted me as part of their family when they found out that my brother Troy and Juan were great friends. They were especially glad to hear of my plans to marry Frances when I returned from New Orleans. Now I would be a real part of their family.

Juan's twin cousins, Leon and Manuel, were in our caravan. Most of their families came to greet us. There were family members who came to meet almost all of those in our caravan. It was quite a gathering; but it didn't take long for the group to separate by families.

Most of the caravan was made up of small businessmen who had gone to Chihuahua both to sell goods and to buy goods to bring back for their businesses. After visiting a while and the group saying goodbye to each other, everyone separated. They needed to deal with their wagon loads of merchandise. Juan and I would be in Santa Fe only a few days and head back to the trading post.

Manuel and Leon and their families met us at Juan's parent's home for a meal. Juan's sister Isabella and her husband Antonio were there also. It was wonderful to see everyone after such a long trip. The families were all glad for our safe return, since we had been gone for over two months on a dangerous route. There was always the possibility of Indian attacks; but other than one attack on the trip to Chihuahua, it had been a safe trip. That may be because we had learned from mistakes made on the trip to Chihuahua and didn't make those same mistakes coming back.

The whole group was always together. We would never leave a few wagons by themselves for any reason.

Juan's mother had made a delicious meal with barbecue beef, roasted carrots, potatoes and onions, tortillas and several dessert pastries. We talked as we ate at the large dinner table.

Juan's mother started the conversation by asking about Isabella's twin sons Lorenzo and Luis who went with us to Chihuahua; but didn't return with us. They stayed in Chihuahua to study at the cathedral to become priests.

"Juan, tell us about Lorenzo and Luis," she said.

He said, "I am certainly glad that Isabella had let me know their feelings concerning a call to the ministry. If she hadn't, I would have been surprised; but not completely shocked. They are both very nice and hard-working young men. I think that God got a good pair when he called them to the ministry.

"The first evening we were there, Lorenzo and Luis went with Ronaldo to the cathedral to spend the night. The next evening, we all went to Claudio and Anita's house at the Rancho for the evening meal. After supper, Ronaldo announced that Lorenzo and Luis had asked him to tell us that they had been feeling a call to the church for some time. He said their last 24 hours in the cathedral had confirmed in their hearts the call from God. They had asked for permission to stay and study for the priesthood. Bishop Garcia interviewed both of them and had given them his blessing to stay at the cathedral and study for the ministry."

Everyone stood and started clapping. Those near Isabella and Antonio hugged them and said their congratulations. The clapping and hugging lasted several minutes.

Finally, Juan's mother said, "That is so wonderful Sweetheart. We are glad for you. Ever since our families immigrated to New Spain in 1790, God has called many of us into the church. I am so proud to have your wonderful sons called now. God bless you Isabella and Antonio."

As everyone took their seats again, Juan's father asked all of us, who had gone on the trip, the most serious question, "tell us about the Indian attack. We have talked several times recently with the families of Jose and Alejandro. It was so sad that they were lost on the trip. And Bill we heard that you were nearly fatally injured in the attack."

Leon jumped in to save me the pain of having to relive the incident as I talked about it. He said, "Yes, I think we would have lost Bill from infection if Carlos hadn't been with us. He had a new solution with him that does an amazing job of cleaning wounds. He used a lot of it on Bill. And once he got the wound as clean as he could, he had some ointment that he covered the wound with. I think the combination of those two things saved Bill."

I'm sure Leon could see the tears in my eyes, so he continued telling the story about the short-lived; but deadly fight. He said, "The fight started suddenly. Alberto and I were repairing the wagon that Jose and Alejandro were driving. The repair wasn't going to take long, so the rest of the caravan had already left. We were going to finish the repair and then easily catch them. But suddenly we got attacked by 10 or 12 Indians. I think they had come up a trail behind and to the east of us. There was a trail up from a canyon that they must have used. They must have stumbled upon us and just instantly attacked, not realizing we were part of a much larger group.

"They apparently all fired their arrows toward Jose and Alejandro who were setting high in the wagon seat ready to take off. Their wounds were serious and they were both dead before the battle was over.

"Bill was hit in the next round of arrows as the Indians spun around and came back at us. By that time, we were able to get off some shots. The brave that shot Bill was almost on top of him by the time they both fired. The brave was killed instantly. His arrow pierced bills chest, traveled down the outside of his ribs and finally stopped in some muscle near his belt."

Leon's description of the fight had almost everybody on the edge of tears, including Leon.

Juan said, "Maybe we had better move on from the fight before we are all crying. We learned from that mistake that we should never leave a wagon alone. The rest of the trip was fairly uneventful. It took us about 25 days to get to Chihuahua. "Some of our families and friends in Chihuahua had heard that we were nearing town, so they had a fiesta ready for us. There was a wonderful meal and a dance.

"Of course, you are all aware that Aunt Anita and Uncle Claudio were there with Ronaldo, Frances and Josepha." He laughed and said, "I'm sure you have also heard that Bill and Frances took a sudden liking to each other. They spent a lot of time with each other. I was surprised that he was willing to come back with us. If he hadn't felt an obligation to go back to New Orleans to see his brother Troy, I'm sure he would still be in Chihuahua."

At that everyone started clapping their hands. Several of them stood up. I could feel myself going red again and decided I should say something, "Well, what else could I do besides fall in love with the most beautiful woman I have ever seen. And she liked me too. And she seemed to think I was as special as I knew she was."

Manuel spoke up and said, "So Bill, tell us again why you are here in Santa Fe instead of Chihuahua with the girl you love?"

Everyone laughed and I turned even more red. I started to say something and then Juan said, "Bill, I know that you want to go back to see Troy and tell him all that you have found out about our part of New Spain and what is soon to be an independent Mexico." He had raised his voice as he said it and everyone cheered loudly. When they all calmed down, he continued. "Bill, I certainly wish you the best on your trip. And I hope you can get your brother to come back with you, when you return. I wish I could go with you and the two of us could drag him back, if that is necessary."

I laughed and said, "Somehow, I don't think it will be necessary to drag him back, once I tell him what I have found here. I have found a lot, in the way of friends and family and business opportunities. But, if you would like a nice long trip back to New Orleans, you're more than welcome to come along."

He said, "I really would like to do that; but I have a trading post that needs running, so I'd better stay around here. But thanks for the offer, Bill."

Manuel spoke up and said, "Speaking of trading, I think all of us were impressed with this year's trade fair. It seemed about twice as big as the last time I went, a couple of years ago. There were several hundred venders and hundreds more people who were just attending the fair. I'm sure they were all trying to find a good deal. And I'm certain they found one.

Leon added, "I thought it was a great fair too. And that's not just because I sold the wagons I took and got orders for ten more. Oh, and a great thing about the orders is that most of the wagons will be picked up here in Santa Fe.

"Bill, Manuel and I all sold everything we took too," Juan interjected. "So, we all feel really good about the fair. There was just something special about this year. I don't know what it was, maybe an added excitement about how well the war seems to be going down south. I spoke to several venders from the Mexico City area. They feel like the war is nearly over. It's apparently, just a matter of time."

"I spoke to four or five people from down that way too," Manuel added, "and their opinion was the same. They said it was all but over. You could hear the excitement in their voices when they talked about it. Next year will be a really special time to be at the trade fair. It will probably be the largest it has ever been. But I don't think I will go next year. It is such a long trip and still dangerous. You can all go and tell me all about it when you get home. I'm certain I will regret not going."

Leon said, "I have been thinking about not going too; but it is a great place to take wagon orders." He smiled as he said it. Everybody knew he was excited about all the sales he made and the orders he took. He would probably keep busy all spring building that many wagons.

Juan's mother spoke up and asked, "Were you able to get together with the family any while you were there?"

"Even more than usual," Juan said. "We had a couple of meals at the Rancho and several more in town." He laughed and said, "I think part of that was thanks to Bill. Frances must have kept asking her parents to invite us all over, so that she and Bill could spend time together."

Everyone got a laugh out of that. Even I thought it was funny. But my face kept feeling hot anyway.

Thankfully, Juan's mother and her helper brought out dessert and more coffee about that time, so we had something else to focus on for a few minutes. Once everyone was settled into eating their desserts and drinking their coffee the conversation returned to Chihuahua and our trip home. There really wasn't much to say about the trip home. There were no problems and the winter weather continued to be far more mild than usual. We all had a great time and were glad to get home and see everyone that stayed behind.

Conversation continued for a while after the dessert. Frances and I continued to be the largest topic of conversation; but highlights of Chihuahua and the trip were gone over at great length also. It was a nice welcome back to Santa Fe.

Juan and I spent the night at his parent's house and intended to head to the trading post in the morning. Before we left town, I wanted to write a letter to Frances in hopes that someone would be going to Chihuahua soon and could take the letter. I would leave it at the hotel with Alphonse and Christine, more of Juan's relatives. This might be the last time I would be able to write her a letter. Once on the trail to Missouri the only way I could send anything back to Santa Fe or Chihuahua would be if there was a traveler on the trail going the opposite direction, who looked trustworthy. Juan's mother furnished me with some ink, a nice quill pin, some writing paper and an envelope she had fashioned out of stiff paper.

I wrote:

Dearest Frances,

Before I leave for Juan's trading post and later the United States, please know that my love for you is sincere. I cannot stand to be away from you. I will use all my strength to get back to you as soon as possible.

I love you my darling with all that is in me. You are the most beautiful and wonderful woman I have ever met. Why God gave you and I to each other I do not know; but he did and I am a blessed man for that.

Morgan and I will fly with all that is in us to get to Troy and back to you. Please tell your family that I love them too and can't wait to see you all again.

All My Love,
Bill

I would take the letter to the hotel in the morning and leave it with Christine.

After a restful night sleep, Juan and I felt ready to head to the trading post. However, our intention had been to stay another day in Santa Fe and travel tomorrow. We would eat breakfast before we made the decision.

Breakfast at Juan's parent's house convinced us we should wait one more day before leaving. Juan was a pretty good cook, but not as good as his mother. She had made pork chili with tortillas. There was pastry left over from the previous night and the coffee was always perfect. And after all, we really did have several things we needed to do before leaving town.

We told Juan's parents again about the trip to Chihuahua. Like many of the people in Santa Fe they had once lived in Chihuahua. They enjoyed our stories. And we enjoyed their company and the food.

Manuel and Leon came by to see us and have some coffee. They were glad to return home. We all had had a wonderful time; but two months of travel was too much. They wondered if they should go again next year. It wasn't usually an annual event for the businessmen in Santa Fe, or it hadn't been until recently.

We had a nice talk and went our separate ways. Juan and I went around and visited with each of the men who had been part of the caravan. We ate lunch eventually at the hotel with Sid and Carlos Poso.

Carlos is a grocer and his brother Sid is an attorney. Carlos is the one who saved my life on the trail. I told him I would always have special feelings for him. He said he would always remember the times we shared together.

Before we left the hotel, I gave my letter for Frances to Christine at the hotel desk. She said she would do her best to get my letter on its way to Frances the next time a customer or friend was headed to Chihuahua.

We stopped by to see Juan's sister, Isabella, whose twin sons Luis and Lorenzo had had stayed in Chihuahua to study at the cathedral. She said she was extremely proud of them. She only hoped that they would eventually come back to some church near Santa Fe.

Juan and I finally started getting tired and headed back to check on the animals. After feeding, watering and brushing the mules and horses, we headed back to Juan's parent's house for supper and an early bedtime.

2 | THE TRADING POST

Juan and I got up later than normal in the morning. It had been a long trip and we were both unusually tired.

We drank coffee and ate pastries, left over from the previous night's meal. We had a nice time talking to Juan's parents. They said there had been a severe thunderstorm during the night with heavy rain, wind, and lightning. That was unusual in February, but not unheard of. They could hear a lot of thunder off to the north, so the storm must have been worse in that direction. Juan and I had slept right through it. We must have been exhausted.

The rain made it smell fresh outside as we got the animals ready to go. There were still eight mules for the two wagons, and our riding horses, along with a couple of spare horses. My horse Morgan and Juan's horse Red were both strong and healthy even after the long trip from Chihuahua.

All our goodbyes had been said yesterday to our caravan members and family, so we got on the trail quickly. It had been an especially warm winter, so there had been little snow on our trip to and from Chihuahua. Now that we were farther north, we may run into some. Spring wasn't far away, so if we found any snow ahead, it shouldn't last long.

It would have been nice to take the normal path up through the mountains; but with our two wagons we stayed in the river valley where the trail wasn't steep. We went west out of Santa Fe until we reached the Rio Grande River. There we rode north until we got to the area of Juan's trading post. It usually took the better part of a day to get there, taking this longer route.

Along the way we smelled smoke a few times. We assumed that lightning had started a tree or some brush on fire. The power of lightning was amazing. I saw a bolt of lightning explode a large tree once. From that time on I was always cautious around lightning.

As we were getting close to Juan's trading post we began to smell smoke again. This time it was stronger than before. We thought the lightning may have started a group of trees on fire.

Up ahead, smoke was rising near where Juan's trading post was. As we made the last climb up to Juan's property, we were met with a scene of devastation. The trading post and barn were both gone. They had been burned right to the ground. A couple of the outbuildings were damaged, but still standing.

We both saw something at the same time that choked us up. Juan's good friend Carlos Medina, who had been running the trading post for Juan, was lying on the ground under a tree. Some of his clothes were burned and he was covered in smoke. He was not moving.

Juan yelled, "Carlos!" at the top of his lungs. We both got off our wagons and ran to Carlos. By the time we got to him, we saw him move. Our hearts both leaped upon realizing he was still alive.

Juan got to Carlos's side first with a canteen of water. He touched him gently and said, "Carlos, Carlos can you hear me?"

Carlos slowly opened his eyes and smiled. He said, "Hi Juan. How are you? Sorry about the trading post. I did the best I could, but I couldn't put out the fire."

Carlos didn't seem to be seriously injured, so we helped him get up into a sitting position. Juan offered him water from the canteen. He took the canteen and sipped slowly from it, trying to get himself together.

Juan said, "Carlos, you scared me, friend. For a minute there I thought you were dead. I am so glad that you are still with us. How long do you suppose you were laying here?"

Carlos said, "I don't really know. What time is it? The last thing I remember, it must have been about mid-morning."

"It's late afternoon now," said Juan. "You must have been laying here for six or seven hours."

"I don't know what happened," said Carlos. "There was a bad thunderstorm in the middle of the night with lots of lightning. There was an extremely loud bolt of lightning and thunder and then the barn blew up. The barn had been empty, except for one keg of gunpowder down in the cave. The lightning must have ignited that gunpowder. I was in my clothes already because of the storm, so I ran out to see what damage was done. The barn was just burning ruins and a few of the closest trees were on fire. I took a shovel and ran to see if I could put the fire out on the trees. I was starting to fight the fire on the closest tree when I noticed burning debris had landed on the roof of the trading post."

Carlos started to cry and said, "I am sorry, Juan. I tried for the rest of the night, but I just couldn't stop it. It didn't take long before the trading post's roof was completely ablaze. I ran back in several times to get some arm loads of rifles and things; but the smoke was more than I could stand. And I became afraid the roof would collapse on me. After that, I just did what I could to stop the brush and trees from catching on fire."

Juan hugged Carlos and said, "Friend, I appreciate you trying so hard. I'm extremely glad you didn't get hurt any worse than you did. You're much more valuable to me than the trading post." By that time Juan was crying too.

We sat around for a long time talking first about the fire and later about the past two months Carlos operated the trading post. Other than the fire, Carlos had had a decent time. There were enough customers that he sold most of the things Juan had left on hand. If a fire had to come to the trading post, it couldn't have happened at a better time concerning merchandise. Not much was lost and Carlos was safe, that was the important thing.

To replace the trading post and inventory would take Juan all summer and maybe most of the fall. It would be a challenge but he could do it. He had friends and family that would help, so it might not take as long as he thought.

Juan got some things together for supper from what we had in the wagons. We started a small campfire and sat around it eating. We told Carlos about our trip to Chihuahua for a while and finally settled down for the night. Juan pulled two blankets out of one wagon to make a bedroll for Carlos. We got out our own bedrolls and we all turned in for the night.

In the morning Juan got up early and put together some coffee and breakfast. It was a clear morning and seemed to promise better things to come. As it turned out, there would be much better things ahead.

As we were all on our second cups of coffee, Carlos asked, "Juan, what do you think you will do now? Do you want to rebuild the trading post or do something else?"

Juan said, "I think I would eventually like to rebuild it, just not right now. I want to gather up what is left and put it in the wagons with all that we were bringing back here to sell. I will take everything that is left down to Santa Fe and leave it all with Leon and Manuel. They can sell or use as they see fit. And by the way, if there is anything you need or want, go ahead and help yourself. "

Carlos said, "Thanks. I really appreciate it. But what are you intending to do after that?"

Juan smiled and said, "I have been thinking that I should take a trip to the United States for a while."

"What are you going to do there?" Carlos asked.

"I think" Juan said, "I will follow Mr. Rampy here to make sure he doesn't get into any trouble. That is unless he turns down my offer of companionship on a long ride."

I laughed and said, "I would certainly never do that. I can't think of a better companion on a long ride. Well, maybe one that I left back in Chihuahua named Frances; but she's not here."

"Good," Juan said. "Well, let's pick up all that we can and make sure all the fire is completely out. We can accompany Carlos back to his place to make sure that his cabin is all right. After that we can head to Santa Fe."

We spent the rest of the day making sure the fire was completely out and loading items into the wagons that we were taking to Carlos's cabin or Santa Fe. By the time we got finished it was late enough that we decided to spend one more night at what was left of the trading post.

We headed for Carlos's cabin first thing in the morning. All was well at Carlos's cabin, except for a little tree damage from the storm. Carlos took what he needed or wanted from the wagons, which wasn't much. He lived a simple life.

Juan and I got to Santa Fe about dinner time, so we headed straight to his parent's home. It had been a long day coming down through the mountains in the wagons from Carlos' cabin. Since we were driving two wagons we had to go slow and carefully. Usually, we would not go that way with wagons; but it could be done, if you drove slow and carefully.

We had supper and spent the evening telling Juan's parents about the fire and Carlos. Finally, Juan told them of his plans to go to the United States with me. They weren't surprised after we told them Juan had lost his trading post. Adventure had always been a draw to him. They saw this, as he did, as perfect timing.

The next morning, we told the stories all over again to Manuel and Leon. We left the wagons and their loads with Leon since he had the most room in his shop and was in the best position to sell this remaining merchandise. We, of course, told Manuel about everything in case he or a customer needed any of the items.

I wrote another letter to Frances about Juan going with me and took it to the hotel to ask Christine to add it to the other letter.

When Christine saw me, she had a funny look on her face, like she wanted to cry. I asked her what was the matter. She said she had something for me.

She went into their office and came back with a letter in her hand. She said, "I have already sent your letter to Chihuahua. And this came just this morning."

She handed me the letter. It was from Frances. I could barely get my hands to work well enough to open it.

It read:

Dearest Bill,

I miss you so much. I can barely wait until we see each other again. But I don't want you to hurry and do anything that would be dangerous. Please get back when you can. I will be here waiting for you.

With all my work at school I will be busy, so I know the time will go rapidly. And I know that with all you must do, it will be the same.

I love you with all my heart, Bill. Please be careful and get back to Chihuahua when you can.

All my love,

Frances

I had to sit down by the time I finished reading the letter. My heart's beat would not slow down. When I was finally able to stand up, I saw that Christine was crying.

Christine said, "Congratulations, Bill. Have a safe trip to the United States." Then she hugged me.

I said, "Thanks. I will."

Juan and I spent the rest of the afternoon telling everybody we knew about the trading post and Juan's decision to go back to the United States with me.

3 | BACK TO THE UNITED STATES

For the next couple of days, Juan and I got everything together that we were taking with us. We were each taking a pack horse with supplies; but we were keeping things on the light side. There wasn't any reason to pack heavy. We certainly weren't going to a trade fair.

We were going to take just our individual horses, Morgan and Red; but we decided it would be prudent to have at least one spare horse for each of us, in case something happened to one of our horses.

The evening before we were leaving for the United States, Juan's parents hosted a gathering at their house for family and friends. It was mainly those that had gone to Chihuahua in our group and their families. We all had a good time talking about the adventure of going to Chihuahua and eating the good food Juan's mother had prepared.

Juan and I said a few words to the group about where we were going and why. We told them about our plans to be back in the fall. Everyone had heard of my relationship with Frances and knew that I would go back to Chihuahua as soon as Juan and I got back to Santa Fe.

After supper and more talking, people started to leave to go home. They all wished Juan and me well as they left. It was a nice evening and Juan and I were glad to feel all the love and support our family and friends had to offer.

Juan and I were up early the next morning. We went outside first thing to get the horses ready to go. After that, we went back in the house for coffee and a light breakfast of pork chili with tortillas, and pastries left over from the night before. Juan's mother packed us some fresh food to eat along the way for our first day or so. And we took a good supply of coffee, bread, and dried meat of several varieties that should last us for several weeks.

After final well wishes from Juan's parents, we were off. Juan and I had discussed the route we would take several times. We would leave Santa Fe in the opposite direction from how I had originally come into town, back in the fall. We would go back across Glorieta Pass and continue east until we got out of the Sangre de Cristo Mountains. From there we would go basically north over Raton Pass, then continue north until we caught the Purgatoire River, which would lead us to the Arkansas River, that flows out of the Rocky Mountains. We would follow the Arkansas River east for about three hundred miles until it turned south. Our path from there would continue to the northeast. Juan had an old handmade map from a trapper friend of his that was going to point the way for us.

As we left Santa Fe behind, I told Juan, "I have really enjoyed Santa Fe. It is a striking town and has some wonderful people in it. And most of them are your relatives and will be my relatives soon. I hope our trip will be safe and fast. It is certainly a blessing for you to come with me. It will be special to have you along on the trip."

Juan chuckled politely and said, "I am glad to be with you. I'm sure this will be an adventure to beat my sailing days. And speaking of my sailing days, I can't wait to see Troy again. I know it will be a long way from here to New Orleans, but the time will pass fast compared to your lonesome trip out to Santa Fe. I suppose it will be six or seven hundred miles to Missouri and another three hundred to St. Louis. Once we get to St. Louis, we should be able to go the rest of the way by boat. That will be an interesting trip."

"Yes, that should certainly be the easiest part of the trip," I said. "But once we get to the Arkansas River and head east, I assume that most of the travel will be fairly easy, so we can make good time. Of course, I would like to make as fast a time as we can. But; we sure don't want to hurt the horses. "

I keep wondering how many miles a day we can average? Considering that on our trip to Chihuahua our caravan made about twenty miles a day on most days, I would guess that we could probably average thirty miles per day. I know there might be days where we would only make ten miles in a day; but there could be some easy days where we could make thirty-five miles or more."

"That's for sure," said Juan. "I have heard the traveling should be easy. I know that we want to look out for Indians; but they shouldn't be too much of a problem. "We'll just try not to get in their way. And like you did on your way out to Santa Fe we will try our best to avoid them."

We had started gaining elevation as we climbed toward Glorieta Pass. We could see that there was snow on the pass. Hopefully it wouldn't be too deep. It had been a mild winter up to this point. We were getting close to the spot where I met some Spanish soldiers on my trip out to Santa Fe last fall. I had expected to see many more soldiers; but that was all I ever saw. Even on our trip south to Chihuahua, we never saw a single soldier.

The fighting currently going on between Spain and Mexico must be much farther south. Troy and I expected Mexico to win and become an independent country. After that they should need traders to supply goods to their new country, since they would not have Spain to trade with anymore, or at least not to the same extent.

Troy and I thought we could do a good job of trading with the northern part of Mexico and I had gone to Santa Fe to check out the possibilities. Now I was headed back to New Orleans to tell Troy what I had found.

Juan and I would be looking for the best route we could find from Santa Fe to St. Louis. While in St. Louis we intended to look for merchandise that we might purchase and take back to Santa Fe. We would also be looking for someone who makes good wagons, that would stand up to the trip from there to Santa Fe.

We will also be looking for anyone who might be talking about their own trip to Santa Fe. There had to be other people with this same idea.

This day we were just on our first day of our trip. We left Santa Fe early and were hoping to get over the Glorieta Pass before we stopped for the night.

It had been a beautiful day with all the mountain scenery. The winter had been especially warm with little snow. The trail would hopefully be in excellent shape. We could see the pass up ahead and there was some snow there; but it was doubtful that it would give us any problems.

We stopped several times to rest the horses and give them grass and water. There was usually a stream near the trail, and since there was no snow, the horses could always get grass.

The area we had been going through was mainly covered with piñon pines and other taller pines and cedars. It was easy riding and the view up toward the pass was especially striking.

Some of the trail had been narrow and we could only ride in single file. We finally got to a wide section of the trail where we could ride side by side, at least when there was room for both our riding horses and the pack horses. We had packed light; but we were cautious enough to bring several more rifles than we thought we would need.

"Juan, how many times have you been up this way?" I asked. "This is really attractive country. There is just something special about the mixture of trees and mountains and a cloudy sky."

"I agree," Juan said. "It is really special here. This is far more scenic than our trip to Chihuahua. This trip is in the mountains. The trip to Chihuahua was mainly prairie and dry prairie at that. Oh, that trip had its own beauty, but it certainly wasn't like this. I'm not sure how many times I've been up this way. I suppose I've been up to the Arkansas River six or eight times. Trappers come this way a lot. It lets them travel north faster than if they had gone up through the mountains. You'll see that once we get over the pass and down the other side, most of the way to the Arkansas River is much smoother than in the mountains and easier to travel. It has its own beauty too; but not like the area we are riding through today."

As we got closer to the pass, the trail got steeper and there were even some switchbacks that would have been necessary for those with wagons. With a bit of struggle, we finally get over the pass. The view at the top was stunning in every direction. We had to stop and just stare off into the distance. It was certainly spectacular.

At the top of the pass, the snow was deep enough that it looked like picking a campsite might be difficult. We found an area in the middle of four or five big pines where it had been sheltered from the snow. The site gave us a sheltered place to throw down our bedrolls on a layer of pine needles. The day had been warm and sunny. The sun had warmed up the pines and the smell of pine sap was strong around our campsite.

The tree coverage was dense enough overhead that we would not want to light a fire. We probably would not be able to see stars when it got dark because the foliage was dense with the interlocking branches from several different trees.

The horses were brushed, watered, and fed a little hay we had brought along. There was a spot right outside our cluster of trees where we picketed them.

It had been a hard first day, so Juan and I ate and turned in for the night. It would be interesting to see what morning would bring because it looked like it could snow tonight.

During the night I woke up when I heard the horses stomping the ground. I could see that it was snowing and the snow was piling up on the horses' backs. I slipped on my boots and brushed the snow off the horses and threw a blanket over each one. I moved them over under one of the tallest trees for some protection. That got them settled down and I went back to sleep.

By morning a foot of snow had accumulated. There had been no wind and the snow came straight down. It was a special sight. Somehow it reminded me of Frances. But almost anything could remind me of Frances because I could not stop thinking about her. I wanted to turn around and head back to Chihuahua. But on this trip, I was not only committed to get back to Troy and give him the information I had learned, I also had one of Troy's best friends with me that I was taking to see him.

"Hey, it looks like winter is here," Juan said. "This is some of the first fresh snow we have seen in a while."

"I agree," I said. "I expected Santa Fe to be a lot colder and more snow covered than it has been."

"Well, I would have to say that this winter has been unusual," Juan responded. "Most winters it is common to get quite a few snows like this one in and around Santa Fe. I don't think we got one like this all winter. The elevation here is a lot higher than Santa Fe. That is probably the only reason we got this much snow here."

"Since the trail is covered now, I'm glad I have you along to guide us out of here," I said. "I think I will start a small fire and see if I can melt some fresh snow and make a little coffee."

"Sounds good," Juan answered.

When the coffee was ready, we sat around the fire looking out at the snow and gorgeous scenery. It was particularly soothing somehow. Regardless, I was having a hard time keeping my mind off Frances. We had done so many things together over the few weeks we were together. She showed me things that she loved about Chihuahua and the area around it. We saw her favorite parts of the town. We went outside of town to see some extremely interesting caverns and we took a ride into a gorgeous canyon that she loves. All these memories kept popping into my head, reminding me of our time together. I wished that she was here to see this scenery.

But sitting here with a cup of coffee somehow made me realize everything was going to be all right. Juan and I were going to St. Louis to get the information we needed. After that we were going to New Orleans and to see Troy. There we would reorganize and head back to Santa Fe. Once finished in Santa Fe, I would go back to Chihuahua and Frances.

Eventually we got the horses ready and started moving down the trail. I was glad that Juan had been on this trail many times before. He had no trouble getting us moving through the forest and down toward a clearer path. By the end of this day, we would be out of the trees. Trees made for nice scenery and I was glad that we would still see them from time to time as we traveled, even though it was certainly faster to travel in the open.

As it turned out, getting out into the open wasn't long in coming. By mid-day we were out of the snow and into easy traveling. We were following a well-developed trail.

From the time we left Santa Fe the day before, we had traveled to the southeast. By the end of the second day the trail turned back to the northeast. And by the end of the third day, we had crossed a river. We weren't sure whether it was the Pecos River or just one of its tributaries.

Juan suggested we stop for the night in a large cottonwood

grove not far from the river. There was a spring in the grove that fed a stream. It flowed down into the river. We got the horses brushed and fed. Finally, we picketed them where they could drink from the stream.

Juan's mother gave us enough food for several days, so we were still eating on it for supper. We made a small fire for coffee. Coffee really was comforting at the end of a long day.

"Juan, that coffee is just about as good as it gets," I said. "I can't really think of anything I would enjoy at the end of a day's ride more than that."

"I agree," said Juan with a little chuckle. And he added, "A beer is pretty good too at the end of a long day."

"Yes," I said. "But they are a lot harder to carry on the trail."

Juan laughed and said, "I think we are close to halfway to the Arkansas River. We have made good time. But it will probably take us three more days. Going over Raton Pass will probably slow us down some. I love this country. I have thought that someday I should paint it."

"Paint it?" I asked. "I didn't know that you paint. I saw the paintings you had in the trading post and assumed you had bought those. Did you paint them yourself?

"I painted some, not all of them. My mother painted a few of them and my sister Isabella painted several. I painted the ones that were mainly scenery."

"That's great, Juan. I have always wanted to paint but have never done it. I do a little sketching but that's all."

Juan laughed again and said, "It's sure good that we didn't bring any painting materials with us on this trip or getting to Missouri would have taken two or three times as long."

I laughed at that and said, "That's for sure. Painting would certainly not be for travelers. Maybe we can do that when we get back to Santa Fe."

We decided about that time to bed down for the night. I'm glad we had been able to travel so fast. I knew we needed to be aware of not pushing the horses too hard. If one of them came up lame we would be in trouble. We knew that we needed to take good care of them.

The night passed too fast and it was daylight again. It had been a good night to sleep. It was overcast and the night had stayed warm. The clouds always seem to hold what warmth there is close to the ground. On clear nights there is nothing to hold the warmth down, so it can really get cold.

We got the horses ready quickly and were on our way again. It looked like it would be a good day to travel. There was no wind and the sky was clear except for a few small clouds. We wanted to take advantage of it.

For most of that day, we were paralleling a small mountain range to our west. The traveling was good. At one point late in the day we saw two prominent cone-shaped mounds way off to the east. They were so distinctive that I thought they surely were used as landmarks by trappers and other travelers through this area. We found a campsite about a thirty-minute ride past the mounds. It was a nice camp, much like last night. There were cottonwoods for shelter and a little spring for water.

We had seen a great number of both deer and antelope this day, as well as coyotes and other smaller wildlife. There was a mountain lion off in the distance at one spot. It was heading south, so it appeared to be nothing to worry about.

After we took care of the horses and had a little supper, Juan and I talked about the day and what he thought we might encounter the next day. He thought the trail would likely get steeper and we might get to Raton Pass before the end of the day. He said we would get back into a forested area; but the trail should still be good.

After we had sat silent for a little while Juan said, "I suppose you have been thinking about Frances a bit."

I laughed and said, "More than a bit. More like all day long. I sure wish I could send another letter to her. But I don't suppose that will be possible until we get back to Santa Fe."

Juan said, "I'm sure it must be tough being away from her, but you'll be back soon. And she has her family there, so she will be fine. And… she has her teaching to keep her busy and keep her mind off some guy named Bill Rampy from Alabama."

We sat silent for another five or so minutes and finally Juan said, "You know, I had a girlfriend once while I was growing up in Santa Fe. Some of her family is still there and I see them from time to time. They were even at our party just before we left for Chihuahua."

"What happened?" I asked.

"She died a few months before we were going to get married. The doctor didn't know what was wrong with her. At first, she felt weak and had some stomach pain. Then she started to have more serious pain in her stomach. The doctor did his best to prevent her pain; but it was difficult. She got sicker after that and just never got better. She finally passed away on a warm, sunny spring day. Her family and I buried her that same day."

"What was her name," I asked.

"Analisa. Somehow, I felt encouraged by that warm spring day she died. It felt like God was telling me that it was going to be all right for both of us. Life would go on for me and even if I didn't have Analisa I would still have a happy life. Analisa would have no more pain. And she would be in a better place anyway, so she would be all right. I guess that's one reason family is so important to me and why my family is so close."

"Juan, I am so sorry. Even with that feeling of encouragement, her loss must have been really tough."

We didn't really know what else to say and just sat there. Eventually we climbed in our bedrolls and went to sleep.

The morning was cool, almost to the point of feeling frosty. I got up, stirred the ashes from our campfire and added a few more twigs. I got the fire restarted easily. We both had a little coffee and got the horses ready to go. It looked like it would be a lovely day. The sky was clear and I saw at least a half dozen robins flying near our camp.

By early afternoon we started into a forested area as the land got steeper. The path had to switch back and forth in two areas where it got steeper and rockier.

Late in the afternoon we got to Raton Pass. The pass was a lovely area covered with pines and some low growing bushes I was unfamiliar with. The view from the top was breathtaking. The small puffy clouds earlier in the day had turned into a gorgeous cloudy sky back to the south.

It was nice to start back downhill after finally reaching the pass. We continued another mile or so before we found a place to settle down for the night.

The horses were watered in a small stream, unsaddled, and brushed well. They were picketed near the water. Juan and I laid out our bedrolls and started a small fire. After supper it didn't take us long to turn in for the night. It had been a long day.

The next morning, we woke up to five inches of snow. There was no wind, so the snow fell straight down. It was untouched by human or animal tracks and looked just like winter was supposed to look. It was so peaceful, I almost felt like crawling back into my bedroll.

We had camped under some trees, as we usually tried to do, so the camp was protected from the snow. We sat around our small fire, had a little coffee, and talked about what lay ahead in the next few days.

"Most of today," Juan said, "our trail will continue through the mountains until reaching the Purgatoire River. We will follow the Purgatoire until it runs into the Arkansas River. The Arkansas River will be our guide for several hundred miles. Most of the countryside will be prairie, so the traveling should be easy. You've wanted to make good time, so this should be our best chance. Bill, we should be in New Orleans in no time."

"Juan, I feel more excited every day about our journey," I

said. "I do want to and expect to really enjoy this trip. But the faster I can enjoy it the better. It will certainly be interesting to see the area between here and the U.S. state of Missouri. Not too many people from the United States have ever seen it. About the only people who have seen it besides French trappers are explorers. And I'm sure there have been a number of those over the past two hundred years. So, what we are doing is not entirely new, but it is rare. That makes me excited."

Juan agreed and with that we finished our coffee and headed off for our day's journey toward the Purgatoire River.

After most of a normal day's ride, the Purgatoire River appeared in front of us late in the afternoon. It was a breathtaking sight. The river flowed out of the mountains to our west. It flowed to the east at first and eventually turned to the northeast toward the Arkansas River.

Small trees and shrubs were growing along the riverbed. The riverbed itself was sandy and about twice as wide as the river channel that carried the water. The water was running fast at this point. It obviously hadn't been long since it had been flowing down steep grades in the mountains.

It would be two or three days before we reached the Arkansas River. When we reached it, I thought we should stop a day and rest the horses. I really wanted to hurry; but not at the cost of hurting our horses. My horse Morgan and Juan's horse Red were strong horses, as were our pack horses; but we still needed to be careful with all of them. A man in this country is only as strong as his horse. If you lose your horse, you are in trouble. That's a position that is not good to be in at any time, especially when you are riding cross country.

We crossed the river when we found a good spot to do so. It had flat banks on both sides and appeared to have a sand bottom. It was not entirely clear which would be the best side to be on; but we had a feeling that the north side would be better. Crossing back to the other side would not be difficult if we needed to later.

The new countryside we were getting into looked interesting and hopefully would allow us to travel even faster than we had been already.

There was a good place to camp not too long after we crossed the river. We took care of the horses and settled down for the night.

From now until we got close to Missouri, our traveling would be across open prairie where grass was the dominant type of plant. There would likely be trees only where there was water. Grass and small shrubs would be everywhere else.

Our first night out on this prairie was cold. The stars overhead shone so brightly that it was unbelievable. I've seen plenty of star filled nights, but nothing better than this. The moon had not risen in the sky yet, so the sky was a deep dark blue and the night around us was almost black. The stars seemed to leap off the sky because they appeared so near to us. There were millions of them. We went to sleep gazing at different constellations we knew well.

By morning, a cloud cover had rested overhead and seemed to warm up the temperature. Juan got up before I did and got the fire stirred up and was making coffee when I finally got myself out of my bedroll.

"Thanks, Juan," I said as he handed me a cup of coffee. "Well, what shall we do today?"

Juan laughed and said, "I'm thinking we should chart a course to the Arkansas River. How does that sound?"

"Perfect," I said. "Oh, one thing though. What would you think of stopping for a day when we get to the river and letting the horses rest?"

"I think that would be a great idea," Juan said. "We can't afford to have a horse go lame out here. The more we can do to keep them sound the better."

Juan had put out a couple of snares last night as soon as we stopped. One had caught a rabbit, so he cooked it up for breakfast. It reminded me of rabbits I had eaten at home in Alabama growing up. It was a tasty perfect breakfast. I complimented him on his cooking skills and we were off toward the Arkansas River.

This prairie was a lot like some of the prairie I had ridden across in the western reaches of the Red River on my trip out to Santa Fe. It was dry territory with lots of animals. I was amazed at how many antelope we saw. There were a fair number of bison too. The antelope seemed to be in small groups of two or three at a time, although occasionally we might see ten or twelve in one herd. Bison seemed to like larger groups. You usually would see them in groups of forty or more.

We saw many large rabbits. I had never seen any like these. They were almost twice the size of the rabbit Juan had caught in his snare. He said he had heard them referred to as Jack Rabbits.

The grass here was short and especially sturdy. With the herds of bison we saw, you would have thought they could have ripped up the grass. However, we saw herds feeding in large numbers on the grass and it didn't seem to damage it.

After two and a half days, we got to the Arkansas River. As we were drawing close to the river, we crossed back to the east side of the Purgatoire River. Crossing the Purgatoire looked safer than crossing the Arkansas. While the channel of the Purgatoire usually was about twenty feet wide, the channel of the Arkansas River was about twice as wide. Neither river was carrying a great deal of water during this season; but a person would still want to be selective about where they attempted a crossing.

We were lucky to find a good natural crossing with a gravel bottom. It appeared this crossing had been used many times before. The banks were low on both sides, so it was easy to get to the water. It was shallow enough that we could see there was gravel on the bottom that stretched all the way across the river. The horses easily stepped into the water and had no problem crossing.

Traveling on the south side of the Arkansas River seemed to be the best thing to do. Even from a distance the south appeared to be the most traveled side.

There was a grove of trees near the junction of the two rivers. We decided it would be a nice place to spend some time. The saddles were taken off the horses and they were brushed. We found a pool on the edge of the river where we could walk the horses into the water. I'm sure the water was colder than they would have liked; but they didn't protest. We would do that again tomorrow a couple of times. They were picketed by a stream running into the river. It was fed by a spring flowing out of a small hill about 100 feet from the river. There was good grass there too, so it would be a good place for them to spend a day and a half.

As for Juan and me, this was a place that we should enjoy too. We tended to forget that we could use a little rest also. This time of rest for the horses would also be good for us. After we left this stop, it was not clear when we would be able to do this again so we might as well take advantage of it while we could.

We laid out our bedrolls. Juan set a few snares. He was very good at setting snares. He had been doing it almost every time we stopped. His snares paid off frequently. I had always thought of myself as being good with a snare; but Juan was much better than me. He somehow seemed to know how a rabbit would think. He could tell how they might move around a given area looking of food and water. All he had to do was just set the trap in the appropriate place and wait.

It had been another cool starry night. By morning it had warmed up some and was the second day in a row that Juan had caught a rabbit. It was small rabbit like the last one we had. It was tasty. Juan kept a small packet of herbs is his saddlebag that he sprinkled on almost anything he cooked over a fire. The packet included: salt, pepper, sage, oregano and several herbs I was unfamiliar with. Juan's rabbit, along with a cup of coffee, was nearly the perfect breakfast on the prairie.

One of these days Juan will probably catch one of the Jack Rabbits. It will be interesting to see how they taste. There will certainly have a lot more meat. But they may be big enough to break the snare or run away with it.

Today we intended to rest our horses and ourselves, so we started by having a second cup of coffee. Finally, we got up, brushed the horses and took them down to the edge of the river for another foot soak. They seemed to like it. We brought them back to camp and used a rough piece of fabric to dry their legs and brush them all over.

As for Juan and me, we walked around the area a bit and relaxed a lot.   By the end of the day, we soaked the horses' legs one more time and brushed them down good again. We had a relaxed evening and then went to bed early.

Tomorrow we would be heading east along the south side of the Arkansas River. It would be our path for at least a couple of hundred miles. Juan's map showed that the river would flow basically east and later turn southeast. It would eventually turn to the northeast and flow maybe a hundred miles in that direction. Gradually it would turn to the east and finally to the south again. When the river turned south that last time, Juan and I would quit the river and continue going northeast. That path should eventually take us to the area where two rivers would come together at the edge of Missouri.

The largest of the two rivers was the Missouri River. It came down from the northwest and flowed across Missouri. The other river was the Kaw River. It flowed across the eastern third of the Indian territory, just west of the state of Missouri, and finally flowed into the Missouri River.

4 | EAST ALONG THE ARKANSAS RIVER

Breakfast was early and quick. Juan and I both got up before daylight broke on the eastern horizon. It was a crisp and clear morning.

There were a few live embers left in the fire pit, so we got a fire ready quickly. It was a perfect morning for coffee and a few pieces of dried bread. The horses were made ready and we got on the trail. There actually was a decent trail, so it was obvious there had been many travelers this way before.

It was our intent to get started early and see how many miles we could make on the first day down the Arkansas River. All four horses were in good shape and adequately rested, so our hope was to make a good solid thirty miles or more. We knew that we probably couldn't do that every day; but with this country as wide open as it was, we should be able to move fast.

We still needed to be careful with the horses. Whenever the ground was rough it called for slowing down. And stopping on a regular basis to rest the horses would be important.

It would be wise to watch for Indians. Putting as much effort into completely avoiding them, as I did in my early trip from

New Orleans to Santa Fe, is probably not necessary. Not that we wanted to ride into their camps; but we wanted to keep an eye out for them. When we saw them, we would do our best to ride around their area. I had a sense that they wouldn't bother us if we didn't bother them. We would see how that worked out.

The Arkansas River did carry a lot more water than the Purgatoire River. It also carried a lot more water than the Red River that I followed, part way, in my journey to Santa Fe. If we needed to cross the river to avoid Indians or anything else, it would be necessary to pick our spots carefully. It wouldn't be possible to cross at just any place we wanted.

With the river beside us, water would not be a problem. It was wise to always carry bags of water for drinking. That would always be our plan. There would probably come a day when water was needed and staying prepared was important.

The countryside was interesting. It was generally smooth near the river. Away from the river the land was a series of rolling hills. The grass was always short and sturdy. We continued to see large numbers of antelope and bison. Last night I remembered hearing what I thought was probably a wolf. I wasn't sure that they would be in this country. I was not expecting to see elk or moose either; but I had seen what might have been their footprints near the river.

Mid-day always got us to stop for a little rest and a bite of something. We had quite a bit of dried and seasoned meat. That was common as our lunch. We had some dry biscuits and bread too. Juan was continuing to put out his snares when we stopped for the night, so that provided us with meat.

We probably wouldn't kill anything as large as a deer; because there would be too much meat wasted. Staying in one place long enough to cure the meat, would slow us down and I didn't want to slow down any more than absolutely necessary.

While we were stopped for a noon break on our first day along the Arkansas, I asked Juan, "What do you think about our route so far?"

Juan said, "I think it will work well. Doing a couple hundred miles this way should go quickly. What do you think of it?"

"I'm impressed, Juan. The trail certainly has seen a lot of use of one kind or another and is still in good shape. I'm with you about it not taking long to make a couple hundred miles. And hopefully the next few hundred miles won't take long either. One thing about this trail that we need to consider is that this trail has been used mostly by men on horseback. I haven't seen any sign of wagon tracks. Most of what we have seen would have no problem holding wagons; but we do need to keep wagons in mind as we evaluate the trail."

"I agree," said Juan. "Whenever we see something that might be a concern, we should probably stop and discuss it."

"Sounds good to me," I said.

After our break we continued down the trail. There were some large trees along the river and we saw one small stream that ran into it. The trees were mainly cottonwoods and poplars. There were also some cedars in places where it was a little drier.

It was interesting how many antelope we saw. They were striking animals, usually about the size of a large deer. Sometimes you would see two or three of them together and other times you would see larger groups. They were always scattered out like they were ready to run, if something dangerous got near them.

I had never been in country quite like this before. It was hard to describe. It was a short grass prairie, drier than I had seen before. Last fall when I rode from New Orleans to Santa Fe, I spent a long-time riding along the Red River. The grass there was short too, particularly as I got farther west. It seemed to be drier here because there were fewer trees than along the Red River.

A herd of bison appeared on a hilltop to the north across the river. It was difficult to see how many there were. We had heard that some of the herds out this way could be huge, some with hundreds of animals.

By the time we started to look for an evening campsite, it was obvious that we had traveled a long way. It was difficult to decide how far, but I was guessing 35 miles. That may have been a little farther than was wise, but it felt like a relatively easy ride. We decided to take it a bit easier tomorrow.

The night's camp was much like many we had had before. The horses were watered and brushed to relax them. We picketed them close to where we would sleep, under several large elm trees.

After a light supper and a discussion of the day's ride, we got into our bedrolls quickly. It had been a long day, so we didn't waste any time getting to sleep.

One of Juan's snares had been productive in the morning, so rabbit was shared for breakfast. A little extra time was taken getting ready to go this morning, since we may have pushed a little too hard yesterday. We felt good about the miles we had covered; but we were pretty sore. I wondered if the horses felt as badly as we did.

The countryside was similar to yesterday. There were spots of antelope here and there, with only a few assorted bison. Shortly before our noon break, we crested a hill and saw an amazing sight. Ahead of us on the north side of the river was a large herd, or maybe several herds of bison. We didn't try to count them and assumed there must be as many as five hundred. I had never seen anything like that.

Since we were on the opposite side of the river, we continued, thinking we wouldn't bother them. We soon stopped for a while and just watched them. It was awe inspiring. Even as far away from them as we were, we could still see how big and powerful they were.

It appeared that this hadn't been one big herd but rather several herds. There seemed to be groups of females with calves that must have been born recently. There were yearlings that seemed to stay around their mothers too. There were also larger males that were in groups by themselves. Some of the young males apparently liked to spar for entertainment or maybe training. The dominant-looking males each seemed to be nearby a group of females with their calves.

We watched the bison for at least thirty minutes, until we decided we had better move on. It was mid-afternoon and we needed to make some more progress before stopping for the night.

It had been a relatively warm and calm day. The trail was smooth at this point, so we were able to make good progress. We decided to make camp a little way down the trail, when we saw a spot that appealed to us.

Juan set his snares and we had a light supper. Both of us were still thinking about the bison herd.

Juan brought it up first. "That bison heard was unbelievable, wasn't it?"

"Yes, I agree that it was," I said. "I have never seen anything like that. They are so large and live out here on this prairie where the grass is so short. It doesn't seem like it would provide them with enough food; but somehow it must."

Juan said, "I've talked to French trappers that came through this country and they told me about seeing herds like this. I really thought they were exaggerating until today."

It had gotten dark as we were talking. Off in the distance we could hear what sounded again like wolves howling. I think Juan and I were both wondering if wolves could attack something as large as the bison. Something made me think they probably could. Even if they couldn't attack an adult, they could certainly attack the young ones. I thought that they could certainly attack us. We would have to be on our guard.

I said, "I suppose we should always be on our guard for wolves. What experience have you had with wolves?"

"Wolves are funny animals," Juan said. "I honestly think

their personalities change depending on how plentiful their normal food supply is. In the mountains back home when it's winter and their food is scarce, wolves might attack anything that moves and looks like food. Here, where there is obviously plenty of food, they probably wouldn't be attracted to anything except their normal food supply. Oh, not that they wouldn't attack a man if he was out in the open and looked defenseless. I doubt that we will have any trouble. But we should be careful anyway."

The sun woke us the next morning. We were both more tired than normal. After the horses were ready and a quick cup of coffee, we headed down the river at our normal pace. Our breakfast was dried meat as we rode.

It was comfortable most of the morning. The trail was as smooth and easy to follow, as it had been the last couple of mornings, since we got on the Arkansas River. We continued to see lots of animals along the river and more bison and antelopes out away from the river.

If our first day on the river had been a thirty-five-mile ride, the next two were not. We had decided we might be overdoing it and slowed down.

Our primary concern on the trail was the horses. We decided to stop once a week or so and take a day off for rest.

After a good solid day of riding, we found a nice campsite. We brushed and watered the horses and picketed them by a small pond that had a spring running into it.

Juan and I ate dinner and decided to turn in early. It was a cool night and we slept well.

It turned chilly during the night. That encouraged us to get up early and start the fire for some coffee and breakfast. We had hoped that one of Juan's snares would have caught us something for breakfast, but that didn't happen. We ate some bread that we still had left from the start of our trip. Bread is lightweight, so we had brought quite a bit of it.

We lost the morning chill by the time we had sat around the campfire with our breakfast. I think the horses were as ready to get started as we were, so we got moving down the trail.

It really was a nice morning, perfect for riding. We were making good time without really pushing it. Then something happened to change our plans for the day.

Juan and I were riding side by side, as we did most of the time. We crested a fairly high hill about mid-morning and both of us stopped. Off in the distance, along the river, we saw an Indian village.

Slowly turning our horses around, we moved back the way we had come. The horses were tied to some brush and we crouched as we walked back to the crest of the hill. It appeared there were as many as forty adults and more children. We had no idea what Indian tribe they might be. We had heard there were Kiowa, Arapaho and Comanche in this area.

"What do you think we should do Juan?" I asked. "Where the Indian camp is there is that little stream coming from the south. It might be helpful to head south from here and go far enough that we can cross that valley and get back on the other side. We can ride that way for a while and get back over to the river."

"I agree with that plan," Juan said. "Let's ride back to the west just a little way, so if there is some dust stirred up the Indians won't see it."

We rode about a half mile back the way we had come. At that point we turned south for probably a mile and a half. There we turned back to the east until we got into the valley. The Indians were certainly far enough away that they couldn't see us or any dust we might make.

After we crossed the valley and had gone over the next two hills, we turned back toward the river. By the time we had the river in sight, we no longer saw any evidence of the Indians. We were especially careful to look out for some Indians that might be out hunting. Luckily, we didn't see any.

Several hours later, quite a bit of progress had been made down the river trail. We continued to ride on to the east until the sun set behind us. We found a secluded camp a quarter mile away from the river and decided to settle in for the night.

The Indians we had seen were far enough away that it was safe to have a fire for a little coffee. Juan put out his snares and we prayed for a warm breakfast.

As luck would have it, both of Juan's snares caught rabbits during the night. So, we would have a warm breakfast this morning and leftovers for later. I had said a prayer, as I got in bed last night, that the snares would be successful. I probably needed to do that more often. I usually spent my prayer time praying for Frances and our families. Surely, there is nothing wrong with also praying for a warm meal.

I got the fire from last night rekindled. Juan got the rabbits skinned and dressed and put over the fire to roast. We shared one and took the other one with us for lunch or supper.

The morning was cool and cloudy. It looked like it could snow; but it didn't feel that cold.

I boiled some coffee and we each drank a cup with our rabbit breakfast. It was a tasty meal. Juan had a way with things on the fire. Besides salt and pepper, he always had his tin of spice that could transform even the skinniest rabbit into a tasty meal.

We headed east as soon as we had gotten cleaned up and the horses fed and watered. It looked like it would be a good day for riding. There was little wind and the sun showed through the clouds only occasionally.

Our day went well. We had a short stop in the early afternoon and ate the rest of the rabbit. After our break, we rode for a couple more hours.

As we were thinking about stopping for the night, we saw an unusual sight. At first, we thought the river was splitting into two different rivers. We knew from the trapper's map we were following, that it didn't do that. After a little research, it became apparent that a short way down the river, the two parts of the river came back together. For some reason the river had formed a large island. It appeared that the island changed shape and size from time to time. This was probably depending on flooding on the river. The soil in this area seemed to be mainly deep sand. That type of soil would allow water to carve the river channel or channels easier than other types of soil.

The area around the island was brushy and looked like it had lots of cattails in warm weather. The grass here seemed to be taller also. There was a marshy area south of the river that was on the south side of the island.

Suddenly, we startled some large animals out of the brush ahead of us. It was a small herd of elk, the first we had seen along the Arkansas River. These were healthy looking elk, so the area vegetation must agree with them. It was fun to watch the elk for a few minutes before we moved on.

A little way down the river, we camped for the night. It was a good natural campsite close to the river. There were many plumbs and other low growing shrubs. Six medium-sized cottonwoods surrounded a clearing where we slept. The night was warm but unusually windy. We had not had much wind until the past few days. Now the wind was starting to be a common occurrence.

Juan was unlucky with his snares this morning, so we had bread and dried meat with our coffee before heading down river.

By noon we had gotten to a spot in the trail, where according to our map, there was a choice to make. The trail continued along the river; but we could take a shortcut at this point. The river was heading to the southeast, and later in what would be normally a day and a half or maybe two days journey, the river turned northeast. We could leave the river at this point and head east and meet back up with the river on its journey to the northeast. Although we had no idea of the water situation along this shortcut, we decided to try it anyway. We made sure our water bags were full just in case there were no streams or springs along our shortcut.

There was a river crossing at this point that looked decent for crossing this time of year. If the water had been higher, like it would be later in the spring, the crossing could be dangerous. The water level appeared to be shallow and the bottom was smooth.

There was a drop off on the south side since it was about eight feet higher than the water level. Juan found a path downstream that let us easily walk the horses down to the riverbank. I rode Morgan into the water, followed by one of the pack horses. The bottom felt firmer than it looked. I was happy about that. But the water was deeper than I had expected. I was certainly glad that it didn't get any deeper as I went across. The riverbank on the other side was smooth and Morgan was able to walk right up the bank without any problems. Juan and his horse Red, and the other pack horse, made the crossing easily. After we had gotten across the Arkansas safely, I took a compass bearing and we headed slightly to the north of due east. Hopefully this was not a mistake. If it was, we could run out of water before we got back to the river.

The first night of our shortcut we had a dry camp. We had sufficient water and the camp was good. We stopped in a draw that looked like it might have water; but it didn't. It had a couple of trees for shade and a clear area to build a fire and lay our bedrolls.

The second day we started on our same heading. The land we had been riding over consisted of rolling hills with the occasional rock outcropping. The grass was still the short tough grass that bison seemed to thrive on. We saw a few bison and several groups of antelope. We were generally too far from water to see any deer.

That afternoon there was a large group of thunderclouds north of us. We could see lightning off in the distance. It was too far away for us to hear any thunder; but the storm seemed to be getting closer. We started looking for a sheltered place to stop.

Within twenty minutes the storm and the lightning were almost on top of us. We were still out on the open prairie, so it was difficult to decide what to do or which direction to go to reach cover. Rain was already starting to beat down upon us.

Ahead of us about a half mile were some trees in a shallow valley. Reaching those trees seemed to be the best option, so we hurried our pace as we rode toward them. We were about halfway down a south-facing slope on a wide stretch of prairie when there was a bolt of lightning that was so close and so loud that it really shook me. The rumble of thunder after the lightning was amazing. It seemed to shake the ground that we were riding on. It sounded like the thunder was never going to stop. It sounded like the top of the hill we were riding across was going to blow up. And suddenly, it did. The crest of the hill exploded with an enormous herd of bison. They were stampeding directly toward us as we were heading for cover in the trees. Suddenly I was terrified. Those trees were way too far away.

We were riding east and the bison were running southeast. They were spread out for a quarter mile as they ran full force away from the lightning. All we could do was run for the trees and pray that we could get out of their way before they ran over us.

Juan and I looked at each other with panic in our eyes. At once we both yelled, "The trees!"

The grove of trees in front of us was the only cover in sight. We were heading that way anyway and had hoped we could beat the storm. Now, we hoped we could beat the bison.

I wasn't sure what would happen, if and when, we reached the trees. The bison could just run right through them, so getting to them might not help much. But hopefully, the bison might see the trees as an obstacle to be avoided and go around them. I was certainly hoping for the latter.

The bison were bearing down on us as we approached the grove of trees. It was not clear if we would get to the trees before the bison. Quickly, it became clear we would not. The bison were bellowing as they ran, and that noise added to a thousand hoof beats, made a noise louder than I had ever heard. We were just about to be crushed into the prairie landscape, when suddenly the eastern edge of the herd must have seen the grove of trees and swung to the south, missing us by only yards. It was close enough that we could feel the heat from them and smell their breath. That was probably as scared as I had ever been. I knew we were about to die, and by the grace of God, we didn't.

We were going so fast that we could not stop at the trees and ran past them. When we finally got our horses stopped, they just stood there and shook. After a minute, we rode back to the "protection" of the trees.

The rainstorm ended as quickly as it had started and the sun had come out again.

Juan and I got off Red and Morgan. We were both shaking and could barely speak. The horses were still quivering.

Juan said, "Well I'm sure I never want to do that again. I thought we were both dead."

"Me too," I stammered.

We both sat down to rest and catch our breath. Finally, Juan said, "I have heard of bison stampeding in mass like that before. I never thought I would wind up in the middle of it. God was certainly looking out for us today."

"I agree," I said. "That has taught me one thing for sure. It's always good to know what is just over the hill. Maybe we should always try to ride on the ridge from now on. Hey, these trees seem to be meant for our good, so why don't we spend the night here tonight? Surely, we aren't far from the river. This place feels right for tonight."

"Agreed," said Juan.

There had been a nice spring along the way where the water

bags were refilled, so this dry camp for a second night would be all right. We brushed the horses and fed and watered them. We rubbed all four of them down with a rough cloth as we spoke to them and soothed them. They were good horses. If not for them we wouldn't have made it out of the stampede alive. Their courage and ability to run and not panic saved us.

Two cups of coffee each and some stale bread and preserves got us to feeling halfway normal again. Neither one of us was shaking anymore. At least we would have a good story to tell when we got back home to family.

Juan said, "You know, Frances would never forgive me if I had let you die in a bison stampede. I might as well never go back to Chihuahua."

I laughed but the thought of Frances made me start shaking again. "Juan," I said, "I can't stop thinking about her. And now to think about how close I came to her losing me. I'll probably be shaking in my sleep tonight. I thought we were being careful and then this happens. Juan, I really want to get back to Frances as quickly and safely as I can."

"And that's what I want for you too. Let's be extra careful from now on. Luck or God or both have brought us through safely so far, and hopefully they will take us back home safely. Let's get to sleep and get some rest."

Tomorrow we would meet up with the river. We would follow it until it bends to the south. At that point we will make our own path to the northeast to find the Missouri River. We knew from the map that there would be a river north of us called the Kaw River. It was flowing east toward the Missouri River. Eventually the two rivers would flow together. Our path would allow us to run into one river or the other.

There apparently is a village in the area where the rivers run together called the Village of the Kanza. Once we get there, we can follow the Missouri River to St. Louis. At St. Louis we can get a ride on a steamboat to New Orleans. If we are lucky, we might be able to get a steamboat somewhere along the Missouri River that can take us to St. Louis.

We were in our bedrolls and having a hard time getting to sleep. I'm not sure about Juan, but I had several fits of shaking before I finally went to sleep. Almost being swallowed up by stampeding bison is something I will never forget; but would certainly like to forget.

The next morning, we had a problem. One of our pack horses had a leg that was extremely tender. The horse was a blue roan that we called Sky. We soaked Sky's leg several times with what extra water we had. The leg was swollen. We didn't know whether this was a sprain or perhaps a fracture. Either way it couldn't be good for us to travel now. However, we were low enough on water that traveling was a necessity.

After some coffee and a few bites of dry bread, the horses were prepared to travel. We took the gear that had been carried by Sky and split it between the other three horses.

We would take it slowly for Sky and quit the minute we got to the Arkansas River. The river had to be close from our calculations.

We were gentle as possible with Sky as we rode on toward the east. There was a series of rolling hills for the first mile or so. The ground was typical short grass prairie that made for an easy ride. Later we came upon a hill that was quite a bit higher than the ground we had been covering. I was hoping that it would not get too steep or rugged before we got to the top.

When we got to the crest of the hill, there was a view that was exciting. In front of us, maybe two miles away, lay the Arkansas River. It appeared as a streak of foliage coming from the southwest and stretching toward the northeast. I was surprised that we hadn't seen it before now. A string of hills must have hidden it from our view to the south, as we rode toward the east.

We were fortunate to get to the river as quickly as we did. But even as short as our ride had been, it still aggravated Sky's leg. It was more swollen than it had been earlier in the day.

The spot where we reached the river provided us with a decent place to camp and an easy place to get the horses into and out of the water. We would probably camp there for at least two days. Hopefully that would allow Sky's leg to get better.

We spent the afternoon soaking Sky's leg and treated it just as gently as we could. In the morning, whether the leg was swollen or not, we would stay along the river to rest Sky's leg and ourselves.

The leg might be broken. If it was broken, a couple days of rest would not cure it. A sprain on the other hand would probably respond well to a couple of days rest.

If the leg was determined to be broken, we would have to decide what to do. I suppose we could turn the horse loose and hope the leg would heal as Sky rested along the river. If there were any predators in the area, Sky would be lucky to be able to defend himself. We had been aware of wolves earlier on or near the river; but we hadn't seen any sign of wolves for at least a week.

I have heard of people shooting a horse with a broken leg; but we couldn't do that to a horse that could still stand.

Juan would ultimately need to decide what should be done with Sky since Sky was his horse.

As we sat around our campfire, I asked Juan, "What are you thinking about Sky's leg? Do you have an idea yet as to whether or not it is broken?"

"I have a feeling it is just a sprain. If we rest the leg for a couple of days, the swelling should go down. If it doesn't, it is probably broken. I'm not sure what I will do if it is broken. I guess I can cross that bridge when I come to it."

I said, "We have been making good time on our journey, so if we need to spend a little extra time here, I don't see that as a problem."

"I agree," said Juan. "Let's give Sky up to four or five days and see how his leg is after that. Besides, I think I could use the rest myself. We have been on the trail for quite a while and I can feel myself getting worn out."

"Me too," I said. "We have been moving at a pretty good pace for the last three weeks. That has taken my mind off Frances some. I wonder how things are going for her. I suppose she is so busy with school that she doesn't have time to think about me or us."

Juan laughed and said, "Something, tells me that she is thinking of you as much as you are thinking of her. I saw that sparkle in your eyes, and in hers, when you said goodbye to each other. Bill, I might be only a trading post owner and not a specialist in love or things like that, but that looked like love to me, my friend."

I laughed and changed the subject to our current location. "Juan, where do you think we are on your map?" He had a map that a French trapper friend had given him.

"Well, I would say we are obviously on this long leg of the river that heads northeast. I just don't know where we are on this stretch. There are a couple of landmarks indicated on the map and one of them is along this part of the river. Hopefully we will see the landmark once we start moving again."

Night seemed to come early. We had kept busy most of the day trying to treat Sky the best we could. Hopefully a few days of rest would get his leg looking better.

The next few days Juan and I and the horses rested. I was feeling much better. I hadn't thought too much about being exhausted; but I must have been. Juan said he felt much better too.

By the morning of the third day, Sky's leg was still slightly swollen; but looked much better. It seemed clear that the leg was not broken and we decided to rest it two more days. Then we would get on the trail again. We would continue to keep Sky's extra weight distributed amongst the other three horses for at least two or three more days after we got back on the trail.

On the morning of the fifth day, it felt good to get moving

down the trail again. Our pace this first day back on the trail would be about half as fast as "normal". But our "normal" had been a pretty fast pace.

By the time we stopped for the night, the landmark indicated on the map was north of us maybe three quarters of a mile. The landmark was an outcropping of rocks on the side of a ridge that ran more or less parallel to the river.

If the map was accurate, we should soon reach the area where the Arkansas River bends back toward the south. That is where we would leave the river and head northeast toward the Kaw or Missouri River. It wasn't clear which we would get to first and it didn't really matter much. Our ultimate goal was to get to the Missouri River which would guide us to St. Louis. But if we hit the Kaw River first, it would guide us to the Missouri River.

We were hoping that once we left the river, there would be a trail headed in the appropriate direction. That would keep us from having to make our own trail. But if we had to make our own trail, that was nothing we hadn't already done.

The next morning, we got up, had some coffee, got the horses ready, and headed up the trail in the direction of the morning sun. Thankfully Sky's leg continued to look better.

It looked like it would be a good day. The sky was clear and there was no wind. The temperature was warmer than usual too. It would be an interesting day. Hopefully we would reach the bend in the Arkansas River and start following our compass instead of the river.

Since we had reached the river again, after our near tragedy with the bison, I had noticed that plant life was beginning to change. The grass was taller than grass we had been riding across since we originally got to the Arkansas River. And we were seeing many more trees. Here, there were trees along most streams and in many low spots. The land west of here was drier and had almost no trees except along the river and a few of the largest streams.

By the time we were certain the river had made its great bend, it was time to camp for the night. There was a nice spot along the river, so we stopped there.

Juan put out his snares and we got the horses ready for the night. It had been a good day and Sky's leg seemed to be doing better each time I looked at it.

Before we sat down to dig out some supper, Juan found that one of his snares had already caught a rabbit. He cooked it over the fire and we shared it as we always did. It had been a long day and the rabbit tasted good, as did the coffee.

We spent a little time talking about family back home and the new part of our journey that would start tomorrow. Hopefully, in a few weeks we would be to where the Kaw River and the Missouri River meet.

5 | VILLAGE OF THE KANZA

Juan and I were both up by first light. It would be exciting to make our own trail today. From the map we had, it seemed clear that the Village of the Kanza was northeast of where we currently stood. I had a small but good compass and would use it to determine our direction.

Breakfast today was a treat. Juan had caught two squirrels. He prepared them just like he always prepared the rabbits. The fur was sliced open down the front from the neck to the tail and around the neck. The fur was pulled from the neck down toward the tail. If you pulled hard enough, all the fur came off smoothly, except at the tail where the tail was taken off. The fur at the neck was pulled up and over the head leaving one a completely cleaned squirrel. At that point, you had only to slice through the muscles of the stomach and chest to expose the internal organs. Those organs were cleaned out and the squirrel was ready to roast over the campfire on a branch with the bark removed.

Back home in Alabama, my family usually did not eat the head, even though we knew many people who did. I think we were all just a little squeamish about eating the brain and the eyeballs, and that made up most of the meat on a squirrel's head anyway. The only meat other than that were the cheek muscles and they were small.

The squirrels weren't as large as the rabbits, so we both had one. We enjoyed them; but both of us thought they weren't quite as good as the rabbits. Juan ate the head on his squirrel and I thought about it, but didn't. Juan did spend more time cooking his squirrel to make sure the eyeballs and brain were cooked well.

After breakfast was finished, we saddled our horses and headed toward the Missouri River. Soon, we noticed an enormous flock of large birds to the north. The distance kept us from identifying them. I decided we should go see what they were, so we took a short detour.

In a few miles we got to the start of a vast wetland area. There were numerous flocks of ducks of all kinds and geese flying in the sky here and there across the area. Winter had been mild and I suppose most of these birds were heading back to the north where they would spend the summer. Some of them may have actually wintered here.

Juan and I each were able to shoot a goose. They were a little difficult to retrieve; but we got them. We would have enough meat for several days.

Since it was early in the day, we thought we needed to get back on our new path. It didn't take long to decide that the route from here to the Missouri River would be rougher than what we had been traveling. There would be more hills and valleys. But if we kept our eyes open and worked hard at picking our paths along the way, it should be a reasonably good trip. Since we wouldn't be along a river, it would be necessary to keep our water bags full and watch for springs and streams.

During our first day on our new trail, we seemed to make good time. It was interesting countryside. Some plants and grass were just starting to green up. And most trees weren't leafing out yet; but you could tell that they would be leafed out soon.

The first night on this trail was spent in a little grove of trees that provided water by way of a nice stream. We got both of our geese dressed and put over the fire. Juan watched them closely and turned them frequently. Juan was a better cook than me around the campfire. He had patience and I didn't.

While Juan was taking care of supper, I got the horses un-saddled and unpacked. I brushed them down and picketed them close enough to the stream that they could drink. There was grass that they could eat too.

I was happy to see that Sky was almost back to normal. In a few more days, we might have her carrying her normal load again. Up until now, she was still not carrying anything.

"Juan, how are those geese doing?" I asked. "They certainly do smell great. I'd say you have probably cooked a few of those before."

"I have probably cooked a hundred geese in my lifetime," Juan said. "Back at the trading post, it was fairly common to have a lot of geese in the area. I've shot more than I can count. And I love to eat them. Finding that swampy area and all those geese was really a great surprise. We need to go by there again someday."

"I agree," I said. "That place was amazing. We definitely need to stop there again. I assume most or all of those birds were migrating, so that may not be home to many of them. They must come back to that same area over and over again."

Supper was wonderful, as I anticipated it would be. Juan and I shared the smallest goose for supper. We split up the larger one for both breakfast and lunch the next day.

Sometime after we got into our bedrolls, but before we dozed off, we heard a group of riders to our west.

We both got out of our bedrolls to see where they were headed. They were Indians heading north. It appeared there were five or six of them. They were just far enough away that I didn't think they could smell our campfire. I was glad that the light breeze was blowing from west to east.

Over the past two or three weeks, we had spotted several Indian camps and several groups of riders; but this was as close as we had come to any of them. We didn't hear anything else and after a while went to sleep.

Juan and I got up just as it was starting to get a little light in the east. We warmed up some of the last goose over a small fire and had a cup of coffee with it. After that, we got the horses saddled and started moving east.

It was necessary to let the sun rise enough that we could see a good distance in front of us. After seeing the group of Indians last night, we wanted to make sure that we didn't accidentally ride into an Indian camp in the dark.

It was a cool morning; but spring was obviously about here. We saw many songbirds and spring flowers starting to bloom.

This was certainly not flat country anymore. Up until now, most of the country we had crossed was relatively smooth, if not what you would call flat. Now it was taking on more of a rough and hilly character. Most of the hills seemed to be running north and south while we were traveling to the east. This caused some inconvenience trying to find a good path.

If we kept our eyes open looking off into the distance, it was possible to modify our routes enough to avoid Indian camps and hills too steep to climb with our horses. Where we couldn't avoid the hills, most of them could just be ridden over. They were usually not steep enough to cause real problems. Coming back this way with wagons would cause some additional problems; but I'm sure we could handle it when the time came.

This hilly area was especially rocky. There were some rocky ridges that would cause us to find a route around them. It was interesting how littered all the ground was with small rocks and rock chips. It looked like it would be impossible to farm most of this ground, except down in the bottom areas.

In Alabama, you could farm almost all the ground around where we lived. The biggest problem there was that trees covered almost everything. You could farm anything you were man enough to clear.

Back home I had two brothers that were still farming where we grew up. As far as I knew, Aubrey and Don were still farming the home place. I'm sure by now they had expanded into a larger farm; but I didn't know for sure. I hadn't talked to them for about a year and a half. Oh, I also had four sisters, Nita, Willa, Janette and Jo Beth. They were all married to farmers, so they were still around home too.

I left home to go roam around and wound up working with Troy in New Orleans. I hadn't seen Aubrey and Don or the girls since. If I weren't in such a hurry to get back to Frances in Chihuahua, I would go visit them all in Alabama, after I see Troy.

On our fifth or sixth afternoon of making our own trail, we came to an area where there was an unusually large spring. Most springs that we had found could be described as trickling out of the rocks; but this one actually flowed. It had created a pond that fed into a stream that ran off toward the south. There was a nice camp site nearby, so we spent the night there.

An afternoon later we got to an area that had an abundance of large oak trees and a river that flowed off to the southeast. There was an area where the river could be crossed easily, so we did not cross before we stopped for the day as we usually did. We spent the night under the grove of trees.

It had been a nice day for traveling. We made good time without trying too hard. The area we had gone through was generally flat. About mid-morning we had seen a large Indian village to our south, as we had been crossing a ridge. We had been more watchful after that.

"This is a nice place with the spring and all the trees and shrubs," Juan said as we were sitting around a campfire that evening. "This would be a great place to settle down. You could build a home here by the trees and raise cattle there on the hill-side."

"I agree," I said. "You could farm down here in the low land as well as having your cattle on the hill."

"How long do you think it will take us to get to the Village of the Kanza from here?" Juan asked. "I'm thinking we should be getting close."

"I don't know, but my guess would be three or four days."

Juan said, "That is about my guess too. I'm sure looking forward to getting to that area. How long do you want to stay there?"

"I think, just a couple of days. I'd like to be there long enough to see if there are businesses that could supply us with things needed back in Santa Fe. Then I'd like to go down the river to St. Louis and see the same thing there. After that I'd like to head to New Orleans. If we find other towns along the river that might be big enough to have businesses, we will check them out too."

"Sounds like we will be busy for a while, Bill. I sure hope there is a steamboat somewhere along the Missouri that can take us down the river to St. Louis. That would certainly save a lot of riding."

"That sounds good to me," I said. "Hopefully there will be one along the Missouri River at some point. It would be great if there was one that came to the Village of the Kanza or close to it. If there isn't, we can just follow the river until we find one."

Late that afternoon, we saw in the distance what was probably the Village of the Kanza. It was too far away to make it there before dark, so we camped.

The next morning, we were planning to get up early and head to the Village. When we saw it, it appeared to be about three miles away on the edge of a tall ridge. I thought it wouldn't take long to get there.

We were assuming this was the village where the rivers meet.

We had finally seen a river to our north that ran to the east, so this had to be one of the rivers we were looking for. I didn't think we had missed another one, so this had to be the Kaw River, and hopefully somewhere around the village ahead it would meet up with the Missouri River.

If this was in fact the place where the two rivers came together, we would have to spend a few days there before we got on our way to St. Louis.

6 | WHERE THE RIVERS MEET

Juan got up first. Light was just peaking over the eastern horizon. He checked his snares and had caught two rabbits.

You would think that nobody could be as lucky with snares as Juan, but he was that lucky and just very good with snares. If there was a rabbit around, Juan would always put his snare in the right place. And frankly, rabbits were everywhere.

Last night's fire had been stirred up and a fire was quickly started by Juan. The rabbits were already cooking by the time I rolled out of my bedroll. The smell reminded me of some of the meals Juan cooked for us back at his trading post. It made me hungry to think about it.

I had some coffee ready by the time Juan had the rabbits cooked. Both the rabbits and the coffee really hit the right note with me. It was a good way to start a day.

We ate the rabbits and drank the coffee and talked about the day ahead. Our route into the Village of the Kanza was from due west. From the map we knew there was a large river between us and the village. We thought that we would certainly need to find a crossing.

Once we were in the village, there would be several things we wanted to do. Chief amongst them would be to find out if there was a steamboat that traveled this far upriver. If there was, we needed to know when it would be in the area next. We knew it would be much faster to reach St. Louis by boat than by horseback.

Next among things to do in the village was to determine if there were suppliers here who could sell us goods to take to Santa Fe for re-sale.

We wanted to find out, if we could, if there were other businesspeople in this area planning a trip to Santa Fe. This was for our own curiosity. Certainly, others had been thinking about a trip to Santa Fe once Mexico won their independence from Spain. The final thing we wanted to find out was any news about the war between Mexico and Spain. The last we had heard was that Mexico was doing well.

After finishing breakfast and getting our gear loaded on the horses, we headed east. As we got closer to where we thought the village was, Juan decided it might be best to go south and come into the village from that direction. This route should entirely miss the rivers, so we wouldn't need to cross them at all.

Juan's idea turned out to be a good one. As we got closer to the village, coming in from the south, our trail went high up on a ridge where we had an amazing view to the west. From there we saw that two rivers did come together just west of the village. One large river came from straight west and the other, even larger river, came from the northwest. The two rivers joined west of the village and the combined river curved around to the north. From where we were on the ridge, we couldn't see where the river went from there. But we had to assume that, as the map indicated, it turned east on the north side of the village. From there it would obviously flow toward St. Louis.

As we rode toward the village, we saw a couple of small settlements that looked like they may grow into towns themselves someday. The Village of the Kanza itself didn't look much like a town, but rather a small village. It was an attractive area though. and being at the confluence of two rivers, you would think the area had lots of promise.

We looked for a hotel as we rode into the Village of the Kanza and found one. It wasn't large; but it was certainly new. In fact, the entire village looked like it hadn't been around long.

The village sat just northeast of and about one hundred feet higher than the confluence of the two rivers. The larger river was the Missouri and the smaller was the Kaw.

Juan and I checked into the hotel and found that the proprietor spoke mainly French. This didn't surprise Juan, who spoke French fluently; but it did surprise me even though I spoke some French.

The entire area was developed by French trappers and traders who came into this area to trap animals for their pelts. They moved up and down both rivers for their operations. Many of the best trappers eventually continued westward into the Rocky Mountains. That is where Juan had previously met many trappers and learned most of his French. He and his family had been raised speaking both Spanish and English; but they learned to speak French too, once they moved to Santa Fe.

My family also grew up speaking both Spanish and English. Our father spoke mainly English and some German; but my mother's family was from Spain. She spoke both Spanish and English fluently and a little German. She made sure her children spoke both Spanish and English. Our father didn't have much chance to speak German where we lived, so we children only learned a smattering of that language.

Fortunately, where we grew up in eastern Alabama, we had some French speaking neighbors, so we all spoke some French as well. However, Juan's French was much better than mine.

The proprietor's name was Beaulieu. He was from St. Louis and had come here to build and run the hotel for family friends in St. Louis, that had several hotels there. The hotel had been finished about six months earlier. He was married and had two sons that were almost adults. They had helped him build the hotel and would probably move back to St. Louis.

Juan told Mr. Beaulieu what we were doing and they discussed some of the businesses that were being developed locally. He didn't feel like there were many businesses that could provide what we needed, except maybe a local trading post.

Mr. Beaulieu pointed us toward a trading post operated by Francois Chouteau. There had been many traders through this area. Francois was the first to setup a permanent trading post. His trading post was on the north edge of town near the Missouri River. At this point, the river made a large bend to the south followed by a bend back to the north. To our surprise and excitement, there was a large dock built on the river near the trading post. This hopefully meant that there was at least some steamboat traffic this far up the Missouri River.

Juan and I entered the trading post and got a friendly welcome by the proprietor. "Bienvenue messieurs. Puis-je vous aider? (Welcome gentlemen. Can I help you?)

Juan answered, "Thank you. This is our first time here and we are just looking at your town to see what business we might do here. I am Juan Leos from Santa Fe and this is my friend Bill Rampy from New Orleans."

"My name is Francois Chouteau," said Francois. "I am glad to meet you both, Juan and Bill. What brings you to the Village of the Kansa?"

I answered in my rough French; but the conversation quickly turned to English. I said, "We are heading back to New Orleans to see my brother who is in the trading business there. I have been on a journey to Santa Fe to see if sending trade goods there might be a good business. I met Juan there and a number of his family and friends who are all businessmen."

I normally would not have been so open with a stranger on

our first meeting; but there was something especially trustworthy and honest about Francois from the second we met him. I got the sense from Juan that he felt exactly like I did.

Francois asked, "So what did you decide? Would sending trade goods to Santa Fe be good business? I have heard other people wondering that same thing; but none of them, as far as I know, have actually gone there. Everyone is waiting to see how the war between Mexico and Spain ends up. And of course, as you probably know, it is looking like Mexico will win their independence."

"Frankly," I answered, "we have been unable to get news for a while; but we were assuming things were going well for Mexico. What have you heard lately? Oh, and yes, I do think there could be good business between here and Mexico by way of Santa Fe and other towns in that area. Juan and I went to a trade fair that is regularly held in Chihuahua. It would certainly be a good place to do business also."

Francois smiled and answered, "Well, as you can see outside along the river, I recently built a dock. And our first steamboat docked here about a month ago. They had some newspapers from St. Louis. A story in the paper said that the war seemed to be going well for Mexico and was probably going to be over soon. And it indicated that Mexico should win its independence."

Juan said, "That is great news. My family is originally from Spain. We have been in Santa Fe for several generations and we feel more like Mexicans than Spaniards. I think, like Bill, business between here and northern Mexico would be an especially good idea."

"Speaking of the steamboat," I asked, "when do you anticipate it being here again? We would like to buy passage by boat from here all the way to New Orleans, if that is possible. Our horses have brought us here from Santa Fe and would rather that we carry them by boat the rest of the way."

Francois laughed and said, "I have been expecting the boat

back any day now."

Francois showed us his dock and we continued to talk for hours. He had grown up in St. Louis and had come here recently to set up his trading post. He thought that this Village of the Kanza was a great location for business. And he was interested in trading with Santa Fe and northern Mexico. He anticipated that there would be at least one or two groups of traders heading to Santa Fe later this year.

Juan, François, and I ate supper together at the hotel. As we sat down, Francois said, "My Great Uncle Auguste Chouteau and his stepfather Pierre Laclede had been two of the founders of St. Louis. They named it after Louis IX of France. My family has lived in that area ever since, so that is where I grew up. St. Louis has grown to the point it is actually a city. There are lots of businesses of all kinds that come and go through there. The city was founded by French speakers and was under French control for a while. Later it was under Spanish control and then back to French leadership for a short time. Now, of course, it belongs to the United States. Many people there still speak French, but English is probably the most common language now.

"I had heard about this area, where the two rivers ran together, as I was growing up and thought I would like to see it for myself. A friend and I travelled out here about five years ago. It looked promising, so we decided to set up a trading post here. My friend, Peter, and I went back to St. Louis and bought a load of merchandise to sell and brought them here. We built the building that I am in now and started a business. It started slow; but in general, I have done well. And I expect to do much better in the future.

"Peter decided he would like to go west to the Rocky Mountains and be a trapper, so he left about two years ago. I haven't seen him since then, but I hear he is doing well.

"I am optimistic about trade increasing here, especially now that steamboats will be coming this way. That will allow me to get supplies easier and more often. And, of course, the steam-boats will be bringing new settlers which will bring even more business."

I told Francois about my family back home in Alabama. I told him my oldest brother Troy was in New Orleans in the trading business and that my other two brothers were farming in Alabama, as far as I knew. I told him there were four sisters still living in the area where we had grown up. I told him about our trip to Chihuahua and meeting Frances.

Francois congratulated me concerning Frances and told me he hoped I would get back to Chihuahua soon.

Juan told Francois about his family and their businesses and their immigration from Spain before he was born. He told him about his earlier adventure days when he had sailed on freighters up and down the east coast of America. He said he had gotten to know my brother Troy Rampy while sailing. He said he was excited to meet me when he found out I was Troy's brother.

It was an enjoyable evening. We told Francois we would talk to him again tomorrow and keep in touch about the steamboat.

Sleeping on a real mattress at the hotel kept both Juan and I in bed longer than we had anticipated. You get used to sleeping on the ground when you are traveling; but it is always so much nicer to sleep in a real bed.

We did finally get up and have breakfast downstairs in the lobby. The coffee was especially good. It was the first coffee with chicory in it that I had drunk in many months.

Juan suggested we get our horses, Red and Morgan, out of the stable where we had left them yesterday and ride around the area. We did that and found a few more businesses that we hadn't seen.

We stopped first at a blacksmith shop. The proprietor was named Louis. He had built his shop about four years earlier, and like Francois, had come here from St. Louis. He did mainly work on horses and their equipment. He made some small hand tools on request. He had thought about building wagons; but hadn't tried that yet. And when he didn't have anything else to do, he would entertain himself by making knives. Most of them were sheath type knives; but he had been working on a folding knife.

Juan and I liked Louis' knives a great deal and told him we might buy some of them from him the next time we were in town. He said he would appreciate that and would keep it in mind.

The next business we found was a store run by a lady named Clarice. She was probably forty years old, heavy with red hair and freckles. Fred, her husband, had built the store about a year earlier. He was in St. Louis on a buying trip. She expected him back on the next steamboat.

The store sold food, hardware and a variety of clothing. There were also, shoes, boots, belts and hats. I noticed that some of the hand tools had been made by Louis. They were made well. I had a feeling that Louis would eventually make more money with his tools than from his work on horses.

Clarice said they sold pocket watches; but had a hard time keeping them in stock. There were several other household items they would like to sell; but hadn't been able to get. She was hopeful that with the steamboat coming this far up the Missouri River the store would soon be able to get most of the items their customers would like to buy.

There were several houses springing up in the area, so people were finding this a good place to live. East of the trading post about two hundred feet was a sturdy rock foundation being built that looked like it might be for a church.

Juan and I eventually got back to the trading post. Francois was busy, so we waited for a while by the dock. Francois had told us he made this dock mostly by himself. Neither of us knew anything about building docks; but this looked well made to us. We were hopeful the steamboat would be here soon; but if it wasn't,

JIM EDD WARNER

we had nowhere else to go anyway. We had no plans to give up on the steamboat and ride the horses to St. Louis, so we would make ourselves comfortable and investigate the local area.

Francois finally got his customers taken care of and came out to see what we had been doing. He said, "What have you gents been finding today?"

Juan said, "We have been enjoying seeing your village. First, we met Louis at his blacksmith shop and talked to him about the items he makes. After that we stopped by the store and met Clarice. I thought she had a nice selection of merchandise for people who are settling down in this area."

I asked, "Francois, what is being built there to the east where someone has started a foundation?"

Francois smiled and said, "That is the foundation for a church. I hope to have it finished by next summer. Our family is Catholic and it has been a tradition to build a church whenever move into an area. That is what my uncle had done when he established St. Louis, so I thought I should do it here."

I said, "That sounds like a good idea. It would certainly give people another reason to come to town for those who live out in the countryside. And for those in town, it would not only give you a place to worship but a central meeting place as well."

"That's a good idea, Bill," Francois said. "I do think that was part of my uncle's plan when they were first starting their town."

Francois showed us more of the items that he sold in his trading post. His merchandise was mainly intended for travelers and trappers. He had clothes, hand tools, knives, guns and leather for repairing saddles and bridles. He had heavy fabric for bedrolls and packs, in which to carry everything.

After that Juan told Francois what items sold the best in his trading post and what he found to be most important and least important. We all discussed the types of items that were needed in a place like Santa Fe; but might not be needed by a trapper along the river or in the woods.

Most of Francois's merchandise was intended for supplying trappers; but he sold some things to new locals coming into the area. He felt that his inventory would eventually change to where it was supplying mostly to locals; but for now, his main customers were still trappers.

Francois said the last time a steamboat came, he heard from a rider several days ahead of time that it was coming upriver. The river had so many twists and turns in it that a rider could get ahead of the steamboat. He said this time he had not heard anything so far; but expected to soon.

Juan and I told Francois that we would talk to him each day, to see if he had heard anything about the steamboat. We also told hm that we would spend the next few days riding around the area. It wasn't that we or our horses needed the exercise, we were just naturally curious.

One day we rode south of the village and found another village developing. There were just a few houses at this point. We talked to a few residents and they said their intention was to eventually have a town there.

South of the village four or five miles, we saw an Indian village, or at least we thought it was a village rather than a temporary camp, since there seemed to be family groups. We saw the village when we were probably a half mile from it and didn't try to get any closer.

Their structures appeared to be cone-shaped tents like we had seen farther west. My guess was that the population of the village would be around 75 to 100 people.

The next day we went east along the Missouri river. It was densely wooded in most of the area. There were some lowland areas here and there that would be especially good for farming once it was cleared. The river certainly made its twists and turns. We didn't try to follow it far before heading back to the Village of the Kansa.

We got up the next morning and decided to head west along

the Kaw River. It was beautiful countryside and not nearly as wooded as the area east of town. There were wooded areas but they weren't as dense with trees as farther east. Between the areas with trees were open spaces. The combination of the areas full of trees and the open spaces was attractive to me. I thought it looked like a good place to settle down to those looking to farm.

After we had traveled about ten miles, we crested a large hill and saw a spectacular view. Part of the view was an Indian village in the distance. We couldn't see the village well. It seemed obvious that it was different than the Indian Village south of town. The living spaces for these Indians had large structures that looked like mounds. There were at least thirty mound-like structures; but there may have been many more. The structures were on the top of a hill. We couldn't see if the mounds stretched down the other side of the hill. If they did there may have been far more Indians than we thought.

As we got closer to the village, we could see there were many Indians around the structures. These were not only males, but also, females and children. So, this was obviously not a hunting party, but a complete village. My guess would be that there were from 300 to 500 living in the village.

What we had seen south of the Village of the Kansa several days before looked more typical, to my mind anyway. They had smaller living spaces that looked more like narrow cone- shaped tents made of hides.

Neither of us knew much about the Indians in this area; but we knew there were many different tribes. What we had just seen must have been an entirely different tribe.

As we got back to the Village of the Kansa, we stopped by to see Francois. He had great news. The steamboat had been spotted and would likely be here tomorrow. Francois said he thought it would stay at the dock for a day or two before going back to St. Louis.

Soon the steamboats would be going farther northwest up the Missouri River past the Village of the Kanza; but he didn't think they would do it this time. He was not aware of there being any docks built along the river farther to the north.

The Janette pulled up to Francois's dock around mid-morning. She was about eighty feet long and twenty-five feet wide. The boat was propelled by a huge paddlewheel at the rear. The captain let go with a long blast on the steam whistle as she docked to let everybody in town know that she had arrived.

Juan and I went on board to meet the captain. His name was Matthew Peters. He was from St. Louis and had been piloting boats for about four years. His large size, probably six feet two inches and 230 pounds, seemed to fit well with the size of the Janette. He was happy to hear we were going to St. Louis. Since they had just recently started this route, they were not sure if they would have passengers or not. We told him that our intent was to be coming back this way in a month or two with much more gear and a few more people.

Captain Peters said the Janette should be here for the rest of that day and the next day. The following morning, they would be heading toward St. Louis. We told Captain Peters we would be ready to leave and looked forward to being passengers on the Janette.

That day and the next went faster than we could have imagined. There was a lot of time spent with Francois. In only our short time there, Francois had become a good friend. We had a good time with him and told him we looked forward to seeing him again and meeting more of his family. I told him that I looked forward to seeing his church when it was finished.

We spent time talking to a few of the merchants we had met in the village. Hopefully, we would see them all again in a few months.

The night before the boat was to leave, Juan and I spent a lot of time caring for our horses and packing the things we would be taking with us. We both spent a restless night unable to sleep, wanting to get on the boat.

It wasn't long until we were on the boat ready to head down the Missouri River toward St. Louis. It would be an interesting trip. I was about as excited as I had ever been before a trip. And I figured that I was one big step closer to Frances.

Juan, our four horses and gear, and I were on the boat. We had made arrangements for enough hay for about 10 days. There were some other people on board. Roy and Elizabeth Selfridge had been in the area to see Mr. Selfridge's brother who was starting a farm nearby. The Selfridges were from St. Louis. Mr. Selfridge was an attorney. They were going home to St. Louis. In addition to the Selfridges, there were three men who had come out to the Village of the Kanza on the first trip of the Janette about a month earlier. They were all businessmen from St. Louis exploring new opportunities. Their names were Arthur Lock, James Bailey and Andrew Teller. Juan and I had visited with them a few times at the hotel. They were intending to start a bank at the village, possibly in the fall.

Cargo on the Janette amounted to our horses, other horses belonging to the other individuals on board, five large wooden crates, and feed for the animals. There was also a separate storage room for passengers' luggage and personal gear.

Juan and I couldn't wait to get to St. Louis. We would probably spend a week or more in St. Louis getting to know what was available in the way of goods and equipment. After that, we would hopefully be taking another steamboat to New Orleans.

7 | DOWN RIVER

After we had been on the boat for forty-five minutes or so, the pilot came around to see us. We had just gotten the horses settled down, once we removed their saddles and packs. He was wanting to make sure that everyone was ready to push away from the dock.

"Welcome to the Janette, gentlemen. My name is Matthew Peters. I am the pilot of the boat."

"Thank you, Mr. Peters," Juan said. "I am Juan Leos from Santa Fe and this is my friend Bill Rampy from New Orleans. It is nice to make your acquaintance."

I stepped forward and shook his hand. "It is nice to meet you Mr. Peters. Juan and I were excited to hear that you were coming this far up stream."

"This is only the second time we have done it so far," Peters said. "But we do intend to go upriver much farther soon. It shouldn't be long before boats are going upriver several hundred miles farther than this."

"How long should it take for us to get to St. Louis?" Juan asked.

"I think it will take two to three weeks," Mr. Peters said. "Every time we start a new route, there is guessing involved trying to decide how long each leg will take. It depends on twists and turns in the river, plus water flow, plus weather, and several other things. Of course, there is always guessing involved, even after we have been doing a route for a while. Our guessing gets better with time. Are you gents headed to St. Louis or are you going farther than that?"

"We're headed to New Orleans to visit my brother," I said. "I assume there are plenty of steamboats coming and going between St. Louis and New Orleans these days."

"Yes, there are quite a few," Mr. Peters said. "You shouldn't have to wait long for a boat once you get there. It was nice to talk to you both. I'd better check with a few more people and see if we are ready to go. Talk to you both again soon."

In another half hour, some deck hands pushed the boat back from the dock and we were off down the river. We had been hearing the steam engine roaring and we could really feel the heat. When the steam set the rear paddle wheels in motion, the boat surged forward for what seemed like several minutes; but it finally settled down.

The river was about a quarter mile wide at this point. It would certainly be interesting to see how long it took to get to St. Louis. At the pace we were going initially, it seemed like it shouldn't take long.

Hopefully we wouldn't be slowed down an extra week like the Janette had been coming upriver. We had heard that the Janette hit a snag. The snag is generally a branch that gets embedded in the mud along the bank of the river. This one was sticking high out of the water. It was small enough not to be seen easily; but still large enough to do damage. Thankfully it hit them well above the water line or they would have taken on water and possibly sank. They had to stop for a week and patch the damage. The boat is in good shape now and not anticipating any further problems.

Oddly enough, most damage to steamboats happens on the way upstream instead of downstream. The damage happens when a boat hits a snag or a tree floating downstream. Logs floating downstream can rip open the front of a boat causing it to sink quickly. There is little that can be done when a tree or large branch hits the front of a boat, except abandon ship as quick as possible.

We are expecting an interesting journey. The scenery should be beautiful. Spring was here and all the trees were leafing out. The grass was growing. There were places here and there where lightning had started an area on fire, burning hundreds, if not thousands of acres. New grass growth was springing up from the roots and turning those charred places green in a dramatic way.

Mr. Peters said there should be a few stops along the way; but not too many. Of course, the boat will stop at night when it is too dark to see the banks. He said they have been thinking about hanging a large metal bowls over the side of the boat with oily rags burning to cast light on the bank. That would allow them to travel on even dark nights if they needed to. So far, they have not tried that.

This steamboat, the Janette, was fairly new, so it wasn't as messy as I expected it to be. Apparently, some steamboats that have been going up and down river a lot over a period of time get dirty and somewhat unpleasant to travel in. But going up and down the Missouri River is a new route for steamboats, so boats on the Missouri will likely be new.

The Janette was a good boat. She was 80 feet long and 25 feet wide. Her propulsion was by a sternwheel that was attached to a steam engine. The steam engine was toward the front of the boat. It was amazing how much heat it gave off if you were anywhere near it.

Most of the cargo was taken off when the Janette stopped at

Francois's dock, so there was plenty of room for our saddles, gear, and four horses. There would have been room for a few fully loaded wagons, but not as many as we took to Chihuahua.

The Janette had a lower deck that was used for cargo and an upper deck that was mainly for passengers. Steamboats did not ride deep in the water, so the lower deck was the main deck you saw as you walked on board. The upper deck was reached by stairs toward the front of the boat. There was a ladder toward the back of the boat for emergencies or to expedite getting down to the cargo level. Walls surrounded most of both decks to protect the cargo and passengers from rain or other bad weather. The upper deck had windows for the passengers to be able to look out as the boat proceeded up or down river.

I am assuming that when Juan and I get to New Orleans and get together with Troy, we will probably want to return to Santa Fe with several wagons full of merchandise to sell. But Troy may not be as interested as I am about going to Santa Fe now. Of course, I will want to return as soon as possible with or without a caravan of goods to sell.

Juan will likely want to spend a few days with Troy before returning to Santa Fe. How we will go to Santa Fe is another question. We could return the way Juan and I had just come. Or we could go the way I originally went to Santa Fe last summer, mainly up the Red River. There are other ways that we could go too. Juan and I could even sail with a cargo ship from New Orleans to Matamoros. From there we could ride our horses along the Rio Grande River, north toward Santa Fe. That would certainly get me to Chihuahua and Frances quicker; but if we were taking wagons loaded with merchandise, that would not be our best route.

And, how and when we return to Santa Fe, depends to some extent on how Mexico's War of Independence is going. I heard from Francois and another person or two, while we were in the Village of the Kanza, that Mexico is supposedly winning; but I haven't heard that they have won.

"What are you thinking about, Bill?" Juan asked as he walked up to me on deck. "You certainly have a serious look on your face."

"I'm wondering what Troy will want to do once we get to New Orleans. Will he want to send me back with a caravan of merchandise to Santa Fe? Or will he want to come with us? And when should we return and by what route? Of course, I want to go as soon as I can. I have no idea what he will want to do. He may suggest that we just wait and go next year!"

"Well, those are certainly some serious questions," Juan said. "I guess that we really can't answer them until we see Troy. But I know how much Troy likes adventure. And I know he has been sitting in his store for quite a while now without anything out of the ordinary to do. I would bet you a good horse that he will jump at the chance to come back to Santa Fe with us. And so far as routes, I think we should return the way we came. It is an established trail and I don't think we will have any problems."

I smiled and said, "I know you are right about Troy and the route too. It will be great to see him. Like you, I don't think he could resist the chance to return to Santa Fe with us. I suppose that depends on if he can find someone to mind his store while he is gone."

Juan added, "I think we should plan on two or three wagons worth of things of value like tools, guns, knives, and maybe some clothes to lighten the loads. We'll want to take the usual barrels of water. I don't think we will need to take any hay like we did on our trip to Chihuahua. There will be good grass the entire way."

"Sounds good to me," I said. "Hey, I guess this steamboat riding leaves a lot to be desired for a guy like you who has sailed on the ocean."

Juan laughed as he said, "I'd have to say that cruising down river in a steamboat doesn't require as much in the way of 'sea legs' as sailing through heavy seas. Sailing certainly is an adventure; but frankly, I prefer this."

It was amazing to me how many bends and turns there were in the Missouri River. It was interesting countryside with many trees, rocky cliffs, and hillsides. If you were piloting this boat, you would really need to keep your eyes open. Riding on the Janette down the river was fun. Riding Morgan would have suited me better. There is just something about riding a good horse that is comforting and enjoyable. Of course, if you ride one too long, it can certainly become tiring.

Our days were spent sitting, walking, and just generally watching the land slide by as the river carried us east to St. Louis. Oh, we did our fair share of eating. Juan and I had gotten some food at Francois's trading post that was for traveling. It was basically dried meat, dried fruit, and bread. We also tried the small galley on the Janette that made a few warm dishes with meat, vegetables, and bread. It was fairly good; but not something that we wanted for every meal.

The turns in the river were always slowing the boat down to a crawl for a while every time we negotiated one. And the boat had to slow down any time a question arose about exactly where the best channel was. That happened far more often than I would have thought.

About five days into the trip, we docked at the town of Booneville. It looked to be an industrious town that had only been founded in the past six or eight years.

Juan and I got off the boat and walked around for a couple of hours. There was a good blacksmith shop and a store to furnish supplies to new settlers in the town and people heading further west.

Like Manuel Leos' blacksmith shop back in Santa Fe, this shop made tools and other items. But it made wagons like his brother Leon's shop as well. He had a couple of wagons for sale and was making several that someone had ordered for later in the summer. The wagons didn't look as strong as the ones Leon made; but they did look sturdy.

The Janette was docked at Booneville from about 10:00 am one morning until 8:00 am the next day. There was more cargo added to what had been picked up at our first stop. Although the boat looked like it was far from being full, it did look more and more like the inside of a cargo ship, according to Juan.

There was another couple that came on board with one of the wagons. It appeared they were in some sort of business. They were just headed as far as St. Louis.

After the boat had been underway for a while, the pilot, Mr. Peters, came down to tell us that he had been warned there was a group of bandits in the area and it was possible they might try to stop the Janette and rob the passengers. He asked us all to keep our weapons handy. But still he doubted that the bandits would try to stop us on the way down river. He anticipated being full on the way back upriver. That, unfortunately, would make a better target. He said coming upriver, he might hire a few guards to accompany them.

Juan and I always kept at least some of our weapons handy; but it didn't really seem like we would need them.

The river past Booneville had just as many turns in it as the river before Booneville. But it was still a nice trip.

About three days past Booneville, there were several times that we saw a group of riders near the river. We were certain that it was the same group each time. It appeared they were watching the boat. And one could assume they were planning how to attack it at some time in the future. Eventually the riders disappeared and we didn't see them again.

I was pretty sure that the pilot was right and the group was looking to attack the boat as they were headed up the river. I was glad they intended to hire guards when they were on their way upriver.

Time on the boat went quickly, which was surprising to me.

I thought it would really go slow. We didn't stop again until we got to St. Louis; but there were several places where they would be stopping in the future. New towns seemed to be popping up along the river and there was evidence of new docks being built.

There were no more sightings of possible bandits, and after seven or eight more days, we got to the mouth of the Missouri River about 15 miles north of St. Louis. It was amazing as our boat flowed out the mouth of the Missouri River into the Mississippi River. The Mississippi was absolutely surging with power. I was amazed how large it was. I thought it was more than a half mile wide at this point, much wider than the Missouri River. Mr. Peters took the Janette down the Mississippi River to the port at St. Louis.

We were glad to get there. It was a relatively decent trip. There was just not much that you could do on a steamboat except look at the scenery go by. That is, after you had cleaned and repaired and oiled all your equipment until it almost looked new.

Juan and I unloaded our horses and equipment from the boat and put them in a stable across the street, next to the hotel. We said our thanks to Mr. Peters for bringing us safely to St. Louis. We told him we hoped to see him again soon. He was aware of our situation and told us that he hoped to see us again soon too.

8 | ST. LOUIS

Juan and I got a room at the hotel. We anticipated being in St. Louis about a week or maybe a little more. It depended on how many things we needed to see and how long until the next steamboat would be here.

Our plan was to see what there was in St. Louis that we might want to buy and take back to Santa Fe to sell. We also needed to check on whether or not there were good wagons and mules for sale. If there were things to buy, but no wagons or mules to transport them with, that would be a problem.

Supper at the hotel was especially good. They served catfish, which we were really looking forward to. It was delicious. Fish of any kind, I suppose, is one of the joys of living on a huge river like the Mississippi. It was certainly a joy for us.

The next morning, we checked on the availability of a steamboat going to New Orleans. The Cairo was supposed to be in St. Louis in four to five days. It was supposed to be docked at St. Louis for two or three days before heading south. It was not clear if the Cairo intended to go as far as New Orleans or not; but if it didn't, surely, we could get on another boat that was going the rest of the way. We intended to board the Cairo and go as far south as we could.

Juan and I saddled our horses, Red and Morgan, and took a ride around the business area of St. Louis. The dock at which the Janette landed was adjacent to where the business area had developed. Our goal, for the next few days, was to explore the businesses here in St. Louis. We needed to see if we could start our return trip to Santa Fe from St. Louis. The alternative would be to start from New Orleans.

I had hoped that we could start at the Village of the Kanza where the Missouri and the Kaw rivers came together. There just wasn't enough merchandise there or adequate wagons.

Our first thought here was to see what was available in the way of wagons of good quality. There was no reason to start a significant trip with mediocre wagons. The first blacksmith shop we stopped at did not build wagons; but they gave good advice. The owner, Gerard LeBlanc, said there were three businesses that built wagons, but only one that built wagons strong enough to last for a long trip. If we started our journey from St. Louis, the trip would be well over a thousand miles. Of course, if we were able to make the first three or four hundred miles by steamboat that would help; but it would still be a long trip.

We thanked Gerard for his information and went to see the business that made the recommended wagons. Andre Caron was the proprietor. His shop looked as if there was a constant flurry of activity going on. Wood and metal parts were stacked here and there around a large smoky room.

Andre called to us from the back of the room as we came in. "I'll be there in just a minute," he growled. "Let me finish this part and I'll be right there." Andre was working at his forge making what looked like a piece of a wagon tongue.

Andre was a short gruff man who, according to Gerard, had been in St. Louis since he was a child. Andre's father had taught him the trade of blacksmithing and had started him making wagons.

"How can I help you men?" asked Andre as he came up to us.

"We are interested in seeing one of your wagons," I said.

He stuck out his large rough hand and said, "My name is Andre Caron."

We shook hands and I said, "Andre, my name is Bill Rampy and this is Juan Leos. We are looking for a strong wagon that could take a full load to Santa Fe and back. Gerard LeBlanc told us that you make that kind of wagons."

Andre smiled and said, "Well, I hope they are strong enough to do that and more. At least that is my intent when I build them."

He showed us several of his wagons and told us about how he made them. He obviously was proud of his wagons and had a right to be. Andre's wagons were strong and much like the wagons we had taken from Santa Fe to Chihuahua. Those wagons had been built by Juan's cousin Leon and were sturdy. Andre's wagons were somewhat larger than Leon's; but looked like they could carry a heavier load. Andre had many wagons on hand. He was hopeful, like Juan and I, that business from the U.S. to Santa Fe would start soon. Most of his wagons until now had been sold in the local area for businesspeople and farmers. I suspected that might change soon.

I thanked Andre for showing us his wagons and told him we hoped to see him again soon. Juan had explained to him what our intentions were and that we might be wanting a wagon or more from him when we came back from New Orleans.

When we left Andre's shop, Juan suggested we visit any other manufacturers we could find first and talk to dealers after that. I thought that was a good idea.

The first manufacturer we found made hand tools, knives, and rope. They were called the Cayden Company. The owner was William Cayden. They made many different types of hand tools. William explained that they try to make anything that a farmer would need around the farm. They made a variety of hammers and an assortment of wrenches, plyers, rasps and saws. Some of them had been developed for trappers years ago and others more recently developed for farmers and homeowners.

Rope was an important thing made by the Cayden Company. They made everything from heavy ropes used to moor steamboats to twine made to tie bundles of straw together.

Knives were a big group of items the Cayden Company had sold for years to their customers. They made folding knives and sheath knives. The knives were as good as I had ever seen.

After a day of looking at wagons, tools, and knives, we headed back to the hotel. We enjoyed catfish again and later sat on the porch of the hotel and watched people walk past. St. Louis was probably as big as Chihuahua, so there were lots of people to watch.

"Juan," I asked, "what did you think of our day here in St. Louis?"

"I enjoyed it a great deal," he said. "I was impressed with the wagons. They certainly looked like they could make a long trip, even if they were full. And the knives and tools we saw were high quality. I wish we could buy those things closer to Santa Fe, so we wouldn't have to travel as far. But, if this is as close as we can get and still buy quality goods, I think it would work. It will be interesting to see what resources Troy has in New Orleans and what manufacturers he buys from. He may buy some of his merchandise from here. I'm looking forward to seeing what we can find tomorrow."

"I agree," I said. "Tomorrow should be an interesting day. If we can buy everything, we need here it seems unnecessary to buy it in New Orleans and ship it here to start our trip back to Santa Fe."

We had a good night's sleep and the next morning got back about our business of looking for things to take to Santa Fe.

There were at least two shops in town that sold rifles and pistols. Some of the pistols they made themselves and others were shipped in from back East. A man named Jules Berger had the best selection of pistols that we had ever seen. He made most of the pistols himself. He said he had heard that someone back East had been working on a pistol that had a multiple shot capacity. He was extremely interested in seeing one of those pistols; but as far as he knew they were not on the market yet.

Mr. Berger suggested we stop by to see one of his competitors, the Hawken Brothers. He said that he made mainly pistols and they made mainly rifles. He said that their rifles were getting almost famous with hunters and trappers.

I told him that we would certainly stop by and see them. I told him I owned two of their rifles and thought they were excellent weapons.

A clothing manufacturer was in town. It was called Hopkins Clothiers. We stopped there to see what kinds of clothes they made. They were primarily work type clothes like most men wore; but they made a line of women's dresses as well. These were mainly work dresses, that were not fancy, but were made like men's work clothes. Juan and I thought this would be a good business to keep in mind. People always needed clothes, particularly if they looked like they would last well.

Late in the afternoon we stopped by a store that sold all kinds of odds and ends. It was like Troy's store except larger. They sold variety of household items from pots and pans to watches and pens. There were blankets, clothing, boots, and shoes.

Another store not far away had similar items to the first store, plus hand tools and knives. Their selection of clothing was not as large. They had a larger variety of boots and shoes. There was also a group of bags and packs. They had a collection of bridles and other horse equipment that were all high quality. Their saddles were probably as good as you can get anywhere.

As we were heading back to the hotel, Juan said, "I think we've seen enough, well except for the Hawken Brothers. I definitely want to meet them and see their shop. But there is everything we need in this town. We might as well get on to

New Orleans and see what Troy wants us to do. He may want to bring everything from there. And that would certainly be all right. But we know we can get it here if we need to."

"Yes, I certainly agree with that," I said. "I hope we don't have to wait long for the Cairo to get us out of here and headed down to New Orleans. I will miss the fish dinners here; but I suppose they will be even better in New Orleans."

The next morning, we stopped by to see the Hawken brothers. Not only were their rifles getting famous, but the Hawken brothers were getting famous too. Samuel and Jacob Hawken were considered about the best makers of flintlock rifles anywhere. They made a rifle that was used by many hunters and trappers. The rifles were light and accurate to about 400 yards. That was hard to beat.

As we walked into their shop, one of the brothers greeted us. "Good morning, fellows. I'm Samuel Hawken. How can I help you?"

"How are you, Mr. Hawken? I'm Bill Rampy and this is my friend Juan Leos. We have been thinking about getting a wagon load of merchandise together to take west on a trading mission. We know your reputation as making some of the best rifles and wanted to meet you and see what you had for sale. And by the way, I own a couple of your rifles so I know how good they are."

Samuel laughed and said, "Going west on a trading mission? I assume that means Santa Fe or somewhere else in that direction. Well, how many rifles are you wanting to take, wherever it is you are going."

Juan and I both laughed. Juan said, "You are correct, Santa Fe is where we are thinking about going. And we really aren't sure how many rifles we intend to take, until we talk to our partner in New Orleans. We are just looking now to see what is available to take or might be available to take in a month or two."

Samuel said, "That's interesting. I've been thinking it

wouldn't be long until traders from the U.S. would be headed that way. I'm glad you are familiar with our rifles. And glad that you like them. At the current time, we try to keep enough on hand to meet the needs of individuals that come in and want one or two rifles. We also want to keep enough on hand in case we get an order for a few cases from a dealer too. So, gentlemen, if you wanted to buy a case or two, at any time, we should be able to help you."

"Thanks, Samuel," I said. "I'm glad to hear that and I am glad to meet you. I've been hearing about you and your brother for several years now."

Juan said, "Samuel, I am glad to meet you too. I had a trading post up in the Sangre de Cristo Mountains selling to trappers as they came through. Many of them carried your rifles and I know they served them well."

"Thank you," Samuel said. "I'm glad you both stopped by. Please let me know if you need some rifles. I would be glad to help you,"

Juan and I told him that we would let him know. We chatted with him a while longer and found out that he and his brother were originally from Maryland. Their father was a gunsmith and had trained both of them. They had both moved to Missouri separately and finally got back together to form the company they were now running. At first, they repaired rifles and tools, but were mainly just making rifles now. In the past couple of years, they had sold rifles generally to trappers and hunters coming through St. Louis heading west to the Rocky Mountains.

9 | THE MISSISSIPPI

The Cairo docked three days later. We had our horses and gear ready to go, even though it was still another two days before the Cairo was ready to leave port. When it was time, the boat pulled away from the dock at 8:00 am and headed south toward New Orleans.

By the time the Cairo left the dock, there were about twenty people on board. It sounded like most of them were going all the way to New Orleans. A few were stopping along the way. Those going to New Orleans were mainly going there for business. There was one family consisting of a husband, wife, and two children. They were going to New Orleans to see family.

The cargo consisted of nine horses and enough feed for them to make it to their destination. There were twelve medium-sized crates and three larger crates. There were four wagons loaded with a variety of materials. A room on the cargo deck held some luggage, smaller boxes, and what appeared to be letters and other mail. A padlock secured the room.

The Cairo was considerably larger than the Janette. The boat was approximately 130 feet long and 30 feet wide. The draft, or depth the boat set down into the water, was about 5 ½ feet. Other than those differences, it was designed a lot like the Janette. The upper deck was used mainly for passengers. The main deck was used for the boiler and cargo. We kept our horses tied in an area of stalls toward the back of the boat, so the heat from the boiler didn't keep them overheated.

John Jeffers was the pilot (or Captain) of the boat. He was a little over six feet tall and looked rough, like he had spent a career in the military. His hair was auburn and he had a freckled face and arms. New Orleans was where he had spent most of his life, he told us. Back in New Orleans he had a wife and two children. His wife, Clarice, spoke French and English and had spent most of her life in New Orleans.

As the Cairo took off from the dock at St. Louis, Juan and I decided that she was quite a bit faster than the Janette. I thought that she ought to make our trip to New Orleans much quicker than the trip to St. Louis. That was especially true, considering that the Mississippi is much wider and straighter than the Missouri. It sounded like the trip should only take eight to ten days. That was surprising because the distance to New Orleans was quite a bit farther.

The Janette had some food available along the way as we traveled to St. Louis but it was meager eating. The Cairo, on the other hand, had somewhat of a kitchen, so the food was supposed to be much better.

We had heard that the cook, named Alexander, was good at breakfast items such as ham and eggs. He supposedly made tasty biscuits and gravy. For supper he made bread, pork or chicken dishes, and a few roasted vegetables.

We brought on board enough hay to feed our horses for the trip. They were probably getting tired of riding on a boat and would rather be walking on their own, as they had from Santa Fe until we reached the Missouri River. We promised ourselves to give them plenty of exercise once we got to New Orleans.

Our first day on the Mississippi was exciting. The pilot had the boat out a hundred yards or so in the river channel and there was more side to side movement in the boat than I expected. I began to get a little sick from the motion.

Juan and I had been standing by the rail for the entire trip so far. I asked him, "Juan, how does the movement of this boat compare to what you had on a sailing ship? Was it anything like this or was it worse?"

Juan laughed a hardy laugh and said, "Bill, this is not even movement compared to a sailing ship. They rock back and forth constantly. Most people who are new to sailing are sick for several days until they finally get their sea legs. At that point the movement doesn't bother them as much. Some people never get used to it and are sick until we get to the next port. They usually would never get back on board the ship."

"What do you mean by sea legs," I asked?

"Oh, that's just when you finally get used to the rocking," he answered. "I'm not really sure why they call it sea legs. I guess it is because it has something to do with your balance. Hey, why don't we go see what Alexander is cooking in the kitchen."

I said, "Sounds good to me." We walked upstairs to the kitchen.

When we got to the kitchen there was a fellow around 40 -years-old coming out. He was mad about something, but we couldn't figure out what. Later we heard that he wanted to buy a whiskey, but the kitchen didn't serve any alcohol. That is what made him see red. As mad as he was, I was glad that they couldn't serve him any. He might have gotten madder and decided to punch somebody or worse.

The supper was basic, but tasty. There was baked chicken and roasted vegetables. We told Alexander that we enjoyed the meal.

Alexander told us he would furnish two meals a day and spend the rest of the day maintaining and cleaning the boat. He said he was originally from Mobile Alabama and now lived in

New Orleans. I had spent a little time in Mobile and told him I enjoyed it there. He said he still had a lot of kinfolks there and would probably go back some day.

Juan and I spent the rest of the evening at the railing, watching things along the river go by. It was fascinating. There was everything from wild animals, riders, and the occasional house, to what looked like the starting of several villages.

We finally went inside and laid out our bedrolls by our pile of gear. It took a long time to get to sleep. I still was feeling the movement of the boat too much.

Somewhere during the night, I got used to the movement and went to sleep. In the morning I got up and went to get some coffee from Alexander. After a while it dawned on me that I wasn't feeling the boat's movement anymore.

Juan came out on deck with a cup of coffee and asked, "Bill, how are you feeling this morning? You seemed to have a fitful night last night. I could hear you rolling back and forth."

"I think I got my sea legs eventually during the night. I feel fine this morning. But it was a rough night for a while."

The Cairo was moving smoothly down the river. It was impossible to know how fast she was going; but it seemed fast to me. We were still close enough to the west bank of the Mississippi that it made the trees go by at a speed that surprised me. I was thinking she might get to New Orleans faster than we were expecting.

The scenery was trees and trees and more trees. But there were some open spaces, along the way, that added a different perspective to the scenery. The trees were a wide variety of everything from ash and poplars to oaks and cottonwoods. The open spaces looked as if they would have been great pastureland. It all looked like the scenery along the Missouri except that we were farther away from the riverbank. The Mississippi looked to be a half mile wide or better in some spots, so we could get several hundred yards away from the bank. The Missouri was wide in spots; but it was no Mississippi. This was quite a river.

For the next few days, Juan and I spent a great deal of time standing at the railing on one side of the boat or the other. We were just taking in the scenery as the Cairo paddled down the river. We talked about our family and the future. And I, of course, talked about Frances. It was a good way to spend time, especially with a warm cup of coffee, which Alexander was good about providing.

In a way it reminded me of sitting on the front porch of our house when I was a teenager. When there weren't any chores to do, my brothers and I could sit for hours and talk about what we wanted to do some day. By that time, Troy had already left home and we would talk about what he was doing, and if we wanted to do something similar someday.

I wondered what Donald and Aubrey were doing back home now. I assumed they were still farming unless they had developed a passion to do something else. It would be great to see each other; but I didn't want to take time to go see them on this trip. I wanted to get back to Frances more than anything in the world now. Maybe we could all get together next year.

"It's beautiful, isn't it?" Juan asked as he walked up from behind me. "When I was sailing, I loved to watch the shoreline. Of course, it usually looked a lot different than this and was only on one side of the ship. Still, it was always special."

"I agree," I said. "It is beautiful. It seems like something you could watch forever. Although, it might not make you much money," I added.

"You've got a good point there," Juan said. "Hey, why don't we go feed and water the horses. That would be worthwhile."

We did care for the horses often. They seemed to be doing well. I had no idea if horses could get sick from the motion of a boat or not. But if any of them had gotten sick we couldn't tell. They had plenty of food and water. And they could lay down any time they wanted to.

"What are you guys doing down here?" said a guy with an angry sounding voice from the other side of the deck.

He was a tall man with a heavy build. His hair was long and black and he had a rough complexion.

I said, "We're checking on our horses and gear. Is that a concern to you?" I asked with my voice raised a bit louder than normal.

He said, a little calmer this time, "No, I guess not. I've just got a lot of stuff down here and I'm cautious about it."

Juan said, "Well, you'll have no problem with us. We've got all the gear we can handle at the moment. Where are you headed? We're going to New Orleans."

"Where I'm headed is none of your business," he said. And instantly rethinking his attitude, he added, "Oh, excuse me for being so grumpy. I'm intending to get off at New Orleans. I have some family business to take care of there and it has me upset."

"We can understand," I said. "We've got some family business to take care of also. But ours must be more pleasant than yours. I hope the rest of your day goes well."

"Thanks," he said.

Juan and I headed upstairs to get out of his way. We took up our positions along the railing and continued looking at the land rush by.

A day later the Cairo docked early in the morning at Memphis to take on more wood to keep the boilers going. It took on more drinking water and other supplies. There were some new passengers and other cargo to load.

The cargo was mainly more hay from farms in the area that had been bought by a broker to sell in New Orleans. There were two horses, two mules, and a wagon that were transportation for the new passengers that came on board.

Two of the new arrivals were a husband and wife, John and Mildred Thompson, who farmed east of Memphis. They were going to New Orleans to see family. The other four passengers were men going to New Orleans to look for work.

Captain Jeffers had told us that he intended to be in Memphis a couple of days; but since there wasn't as much to load, as he expected we only stayed there one day. The next morning, we were on our way again.

It sounded as if we were a little less than halfway to New Orleans. I was getting more and more excited to see Troy and tell him about my trip to Santa Fe and Chihuahua and Frances. And I was even more anxious about turning around and heading back to see Frances in Chihuahua, as soon as possible.

Juan was also looking forward to getting to New Orleans and seeing Troy. They had not seen each other since their sailing days when they worked together on several ships. Those ships had been carrying cargo up and down the east coast of the United States.

Their mutual interests in adventure had taken them both from their homes, Juan in Santa Fe and Troy in East Alabama, to the East Coast of the United States where they met and became great friends. Traveling up and down the coast for almost a year had given them time to know each other well. Then they went their separate ways. Juan went home to Santa Fe and Troy decided to stay in New Orleans.

When I left New Orleans for Santa Fe almost a year ago, Troy suggested that I try to find Juan and I had. In fact, we had become good friends too. Now he was coming back to New Orleans with me to see Troy.

I had gone to Santa Fe originally because Troy and I had thought that it might be a good place to sell a wide variety of merchandise. At the time, Spain controlled that territory and was in a war with Mexico which wanted its independence. We thought that once Mexico won its independence it would welcome traders from the United States.

Juan and I had not heard anything about the war recently; but everything we had heard in the last year led us to believe

Mexico would win its independence.

For most of our trip down both the Missouri River, and now the Mississippi River, the weather had been almost perfect. That suddenly changed with a storm that started rough and got worse.

The wind acted as if it wanted to blow the Cairo over. Captain Jeffers tried to get the boat closer to the shore where he could find shelter. Hard gusts of wind were blowing from the west. Our hope was to get closer to tall trees on the western shore of the river. He asked several of the passengers to keep an eye out on the side of the boat for any snags. We did the best we could but the rain was coming down so hard that it was difficult to see. It was late in the day. The sun was still up and we would have been able to see well without the storm. As it was, we could barely see a thing. Captain Jeffers was able to get the Cairo close enough to the shore that the boat did have some shelter.

The rain and heavy lightning continued for a while. Eventually we got out of the worst of the storm as it moved on to the east. A string of tall trees along the bank had given us protection just long enough to get through the worst of the storm. As the storm passed over, Captain Jeffers piloted the Cairo farther out in the river. That certainly was a good thing because streams feeding into the river came rushing at full force into the river. One stream could have done serious damage to the Cairo, if we had been closer to it as we passed by. It was flushing dead trees and branches out into the river and could have pushed them right into the side of the boat.

After thirty minutes, we had gotten by the worst of the storm and its aftermath. By looking at the bank of the river, we could tell the river was running quite a bit higher than it had before the rain. The land along most of the river was extremely flat and stretched out for several miles on both sides. It appeared this land could flood badly in rainy years.

That afternoon, Juan and I went to care for our horses and bumped into the man who had gotten angry with us earlier. He was with the man who had previously gotten angry because the kitchen could not sell him a whiskey. The two men were yelling at each other and had almost come to blows until we got there. Somehow, just the presence of other people seemed to calm them down. They abruptly finished their conversation, if that's what it was, and went on their individual ways.

I assumed that the man who had yelled at us, had yelled at the other man, because he was in the cargo area like we had been. We found out later that the man who yelled at us was Mr. Thomas and the other man was Mr. Jenkins.

I think we were all a little more on edge after the storm. And the trip had begun to drag. I think Juan and I were feeling as much as anybody else. But we were also thinking that New Orleans was not far away.

By midmorning the next day, we reached New Orleans to everyone's relief. Juan and I were even more excited than usual. Once the Cairo reached its dock and got tied up, Captain Jeffers blew the boat's whistle to let us know we could gather our horses and equipment and begin to leave the boat. That whistle was amazingly loud. Since the whistle got its power from the steam engine, there seemed to be no end to it. It could literally blow forever as long as the engine was generating steam.

Juan and I found Captain Jeffers and thanked him for the trip. We told him that we hoped to see him again soon. He said he intended to spend about a week at his home, here in New Orleans, and would head back north in a little over a week.

We spoke to several of the other people on the boat and said goodbye to them.

The horses were certainly ready to get off the boat. When we got the gear and horses off the boat, the horses practically wanted to dance with excitement. It was tough to control them for a few minutes; but they did finally get back to normal.

Once we got our land legs back and I got my bearings, we headed toward Troy's store.

10 | TROY

It was almost noon when we stopped in front of Troy's store. There was a new sign saying Rampy Mercantile and Hardware. It was much bigger than the old sign and more brightly painted. And I could tell that Troy had added on his building. That looked like a good sign.

In all the time I was gone I hadn't thought too much about how Troy was doing. He had always been a busy guy that worked hard. I just assumed he would do well. That is one reason his thoughts about business in Santa Fe had stuck with me. He thought it was a good idea, so I thought it was a good idea. I couldn't wait to see him. I felt like running into the building. I'm glad I didn't because there was a shock waiting for me there.

Juan and I walked into the store together with Juan walking in first. Inside there were several people looking around. I could see Troy in the back of the store talking to two customers. As we walked toward Troy, the two customers turned around part way and I had to stop to catch my breath. They were our other two brothers, Aubrey and Donald. They looked a few years older than the last time I saw them; but it was them.

About that time Troy looked toward Juan and me. For a second, he had a surprised look on his face. He said something to Aubrey and Donald and rushed over to us. He gave me a huge hug which took my breath away again. Juan grabbed Troy and gave him a big hug. By that time, Aubrey and Donald realized what was going on and rushed over to join our wrestling match. It was a wonderful reunion. Frankly it made us all cry… in a manly sort of way, of course.

Troy spoke first. "It's about time you got back. How have you been? And how on earth did you get Juan to come with you?"

"Well, it's all a pretty long story," I said. "Why don't you close for lunch, so Juan and I can tell you all about it. And you can tell me how these two got here."

Troy didn't close. He just turned everything over to an assistant and we headed out for lunch. There was a new café just across the street, so we ate there.

After we ordered, I asked, "So, Aubrey and Donald, what brought you here to see Troy?

They both laughed and Aubrey spoke first. "Well, Donald and I have been farming together for the past two years. We have some friends that help us. This spring we came up with the idea of planting our crops as early as we could and then turning them over to our friends. They will cultivate as needed, and even harvest if we aren't back in time. After that we came here to spend some time with you and Troy. Troy told us you had gone west for a while and would be back eventually; but he didn't know when."

Troy said, "They got here about two months ago and have been a lot of help. They were here in time to help me with the expansion you no doubt saw on your way into the store."

"Yes, we saw the expansion," I said. "It looks great. You must be doing well."

Troy chuckled and said, "Yes, things are going well. So, tell us about your adventure. I told the guys about your trip out west to explore trading in the Santa Fe area. What did you find out? But first, how have you been?"

I smiled and said, "I've been wonderful! And I have found that Santa Fe and Chihuahua would both be good markets."

Juan jumped in and said, "And he fell in love with one of my cousins in Chihuahua."

"Well, that is true," I added. "I couldn't resist. She was stunning and intelligent and friendly and loving and …"

"I think we get the picture," Troy said. "What's her name?"

"Frances Leos," I said. "And with that in mind, I told her I would try to get back to Chihuahua as soon as I possibly could. So, I'm hoping if you guys would like a little adventure, we could take a few wagons full of merchandise to Santa Fe. Not that I'm anxious or anything. But, if you are interested, I think we should plan the trip and head west."

"Wow, you certainly sound anxious enough," Troy said with a smile. "I think we should do some serious planning on that. A new business venture always sounds like a good deal. But first we all want some details as to what you have done this past year."

"Well, it's quite a long story," I said. "So maybe we should order some more coffee to keep you guys awake."

Troy said, "You don't have to tell us everything. How about just telling us the basics?"

"Ok, so here goes," I said. Looking first at Donald and Aubrey, I started. "I left here on my horse Morgan with two pack horses loaded with some trade items. Mainly I took some knives and hand tools. I rode a ferry across the Mississippi River and went west until I got to the Atchafalaya River. I followed it north to the Red River. My plan was to follow the Red River west about as far as it would go. Once that ran out, I just kept going west until I got to Santa Fe.

"As I was going across land belonging both to various Indian tribes and the country of Spain, it was clear that the countryside wouldn't be deserted. I tried my best to avoid both groups as often as possible.

"I did have two brushes with different Indian tribes. Other than losing the pack horses and most of the trade goods, everything was all right.

"When I finally got into the Sangre de Cristo Mountains, I ran into some Spanish soldiers for the first time. Since I hadn't seen any before that, I assumed most Spanish soldiers were involved in the war with Mexico somewhere else.

"Hey, what have you heard about that, Troy? Is it still likely that Mexico will win their independence?"

"It sounds like the war is almost over and Mexico is winning," Troy said. "So, carry on. How did you find Juan? I have told Donald and Aubrey all about meeting and working with Juan. Juan, you might want to tell them the story yourself someday to make sure I told it right."

I continued, "Once I got to Santa Fe, I stopped and got a room at the hotel. It just so happened that some of Juan's relatives owned and ran the hotel. They told me that Juan had a trading post up north of Santa Fe toward Taos. We got together and he told me he would give me a place to live if I would help him for a while. That sounded like a good idea, so we worked together for several months. My intent in going to Santa Fe was to learn about the area's need for trading partners in the U.S. Working with Juan really was perfect. So anyway, that's how I got to Santa Fe and got to know Juan."

Aubrey said, "Tell us how you met Juan's cousin."

"Well, there is a big trade fair every year in Chihuahua," I started. "Juan invited me to go, so I did. There were several groups of businessmen going from Santa Fe. Juan got a group of friends and family together to go to Chihuahua by caravan. The final count was thirty-four men, sixty mules, thirty-eight horses and fifteen wagons. That was after we joined with another group for protection. We wanted a large number of men for safety. It was possible that we could be attacked by Indians or bandits from rumors we had been hearing."

Juan jumped into the conversation and said, "Bill, I know you probably don't want to mention it; but you should probably tell them about how you almost died. Remember, they are family and should know about that type of thing."

"I know you're right, Juan," I said. "But it is just difficult to talk about." Everyone was looking at me with their eyes open wide, so I continued. "Well, this is hard for me to talk about, because I don't want to think about it. A small part of our caravan was separated from the main caravan, while a repair was being made on a wagon. A group of young Indian braves happened along, at just the wrong time. They attacked us, not knowing we were part of a larger caravan that was not far away. I was hit in the chest by an arrow that did a fair bit of damage. There were two other men in our group, Jose and Alejandro, that were killed. I obviously feel much worse about Jose and Alejandro than I do myself because I survived and they didn't.

"We had a man named Carlos Poso with us who had been trained in medical procedures as a soldier in the Spanish Army. He treated me for three or four weeks until I got better. I don't think I would have survived without him. You will meet Carlos when we get to Santa Fe. So, when you meet him, shake his hand and thank him for saving your brother's life."

My brothers all had shocked looks on their faces, so I continued with my stories of the trip to Chihuahua. I told them about the rest of the caravan, the trade fair, and meeting Frances and her family.

I said, "When we got to Chihuahua, there was a big party welcoming us and others to town. At the party Juan introduced me to his Aunt Anita, Uncle Claudio, and their two daughters. The oldest daughter, Frances, had just finished several years of schooling in Mexico City. She had returned to Chihuahua to teach school at the cathedral. They have a regular school there, plus a school for priests. Frances's brother, Ronaldo, is in school to become a priest. He is close to being finished. Or by now he may be finished. Oh, and the other sister is Josepha. She is finished with school locally and trying to decide what to do next."

"Why didn't you bring Frances here with you," Troy asked?

"I just didn't think we had had enough time together," I said. "I couldn't just ask her to marry me after we had known each other a total of three weeks and take her away from her family back to the U.S. I told her that I had to get back here and tell you all that I had found out and all that I had done. I told her it was my obligation. I promised to be back to see her as fast as I could. I told her it might be as much as a year. She said she would wait for me."

"Wow, so you left Frances behind just so you could report back to me?" Troy asked.

"Of course," I said. "I told you I would do it, so I had to do it."

"Brother, I certainly admire your tenacity and your character," Troy said. "We need to figure out a way for you to get back to Chihuahua and to Frances as fast as we can. And, if we can make a little money along the way, that would be good too."

"I agree completely," I said. "Why don't Juan and I spend a few days here relaxing after our trip from Santa Fe? We can all discuss our return later. And, Troy, in the meantime you can fill Juan and I in on your business here. It looks like you have made lots of changes besides your building addition. And later, maybe you can show us around town."

That's exactly what Troy did. He spent the rest of the day going over his business operation with us. It was more complex than it had been a year ago. He had taken on two partners that had invested in the store. Together they had started several additional operations. Those included building cargo wagons and manufacturing several metal items such as hand tools and knives. It was a lot like the things that Manuel and Leon were doing back in Santa Fe, but on a bigger scale.

I was impressed with Troy's expanding business. I wondered if he would be too busy to go with us back to Santa Fe. And I was wondering what Aubrey's and Donald's intentions were. Hopefully they would be up for an adventure. I told myself I should relax for a few days and we would discuss those things when the time was right. And it only seemed right to let Troy and Juan get reacquainted and talk about old and new times.

Troy introduced us to his partners. Albert McClean was mainly working in the store and Ralph Miller oversaw their manufacturing operations. They had both been born somewhere in the Carolinas. Albert was probably Troy's age and Ralph was around my age. Albert and Ralph both grew up along the coast and had done a fair bit of sailing before they met each other and became friends.

Albert suggested they both go to New Orleans to see what it was like. Their intention was to return to the Carolinas; but that had not happened. They both had grown to like New Orleans too much to leave. They had been here two years before they met Troy and started working with him in his business. Albert married a local young lady named Sierra. Ralph was not married.

By the time we learned all about Troy's business it was starting to get late. Troy took us across the street again for supper. We talked more and finally went to his house. It was only a few blocks away. There was room for all of us to stay with him. Aubrey and Donald had been staying there since they came to town. He had a corral behind the house where we kept our four horses.

It had been a great day! I was so glad to finally get back to New Orleans and see Troy. And for me to see both Aubrey and Donald, was completely unexpected and shocking; but wonderful.

The next morning, we all saddled our horses to ride around. Morgan and Red seemed to be happy to be out of the corral and moving around. They had spent weeks riding on two different steamboats doing nothing, so I could understand how they were both feeling.

Troy took us first to his manufacturing operation that was several blocks away. Ralph Miller was there to show us around. He showed us how they were making wagons. The wagons were similar to those Leon made back in Santa Fe. They were a bit larger, but generally made the same, even down to the flat blade springs. It appeared they could make a long trip without much in the way of problems.

Ralph showed us some of the hand tools and other items made in their shop. They were keeping several men employed on each operation.

After our tour of the shops, we rode around the area. South of where Troy lived and had his shops there were lots of low-lying area that looked as if it could flood easily. The Mississippi nearby carried so much water that it was inevitable to also carry tons of soil with it. Over the years the dirt had made the delta that we were seeing. It probably stretched out for miles.

We rode north through the main part of town that wasn't far from Troy's shop. It looked as if there were mainly new businesses in this area. We did see some older businesses and churches, but not many. Troy had told me there was a lot more to town. There were many older homes and businesses north of the town square.

The town square had a large building in the middle of it that turned out to be the parish courthouse. As we rode past, a man coming out of the courthouse waved at Troy and yelled, "Hi Troy." Troy told us later that this was Dan Edwards, the local sheriff.

We continued our ride north until we reached the edge of town. The town was much larger than I had realized. There was a road that continued north; but we turned west and rode back along the river. After a while we stopped for lunch at a bar by the river.

The bar was empty except for the five of us. I was surprised how spicy but tasty the food was. Donald and Aubrey had shrimp etouffee. Troy had gumbo and I had jambalaya. We all had a beer with our lunch and another one after lunch just to cool off the heat in our mouths.

Troy was laughing at us as we tried to cool off. He had eaten here before and knew the food was spicy.

"How did you guys like the food?" Troy asked. "It's pretty spicy; but you would learn to love it, if you lived here long enough. The people in this area that are called Cajuns make this style of food and it's always hot. I love it."

Donald said, "I would have to admit that it was tasty; but I would have a hard time getting used to the heat that comes with it."

Aubrey added, "Me too. That was especially spicy."

Juan and I didn't have much to say. It was certainly spicy; but we had eaten food that was hotter. It was plenty good though.

Later as we rode back past the Courthouse, we just happened to see the Sheriff again. He called for us to stop.

He asked, "Were any of you fellows on the Cairo when it came in yesterday morning?"

I said, "Juan and I were."

Troy told the Sheriff that I was his brother and Juan was a close friend. Juan and I both shook hands with the Sheriff.

Juan asked, "Was there a problem of some kind?" He could tell from the Sheriff's tone that he was concerned about something.

The Sheriff said, "Well there was a man found dead this morning. He supposedly was on the Cairo when it came into town. Could you look at the body and see if you can identify him?"

"Sure, Sheriff, we would be willing to do that," I said.

The body was still lying where it had been found. It was Mr. Thomas, the man that had yelled at us one evening on the Cairo while we were checking our gear. We told the Sheriff that we had talked to him once, but hadn't asked his first name. We explained that he seemed to be unusually concerned about the safety of his gear. I told him that Mr. Thomas had had an argument on the boat with a Mr. Jenkins; but that was all we knew. The Sheriff thanked us for the information and we continued on our way. It was getting late, so we all headed back to Troy's shop to help him close for the day.

The next day Juan and I decided we would enjoy staying at Troy's store and helping there. It was a good day and a lot of fun. There were many people that came and went in a day's time. It was not like Juan's trading post at all. Juan might not have more than a dozen customers in a week. Oh, but Juan did enjoy his trading post and did make some money from the merchandise he sold.

Toward the end of the day, Juan said, "Wow, if I had this much business back at my trading post I just wouldn't know what to do. But this was fun. I'm glad we got the opportunity to work here."

I was glad we worked here too. It certainly wasn't what I was used to either. I thought we should help Troy for another week or two. After that, we could start talking about heading back to Santa Fe.

Two weeks later the five of us sat down for supper and I brought up the idea of going to Santa Fe. It had been nice getting back together with my brothers; but the time was right to head back to Chihuahua and Frances.

I said, "I've really enjoyed the past few weeks here and it has been great seeing all of you; but I'm thinking I need to head back to Chihuahua as soon as I can. Juan and I have talked it over and we are ready to get on the road to Santa Fe. I'm wondering if any of you would like to go with us. All of you at one time or the other have expressed some interest in going; but who of you is really interested?" I let that question hang in the air.

After a minute Troy said, "Well, since this project was originally my idea, I'd have to say that I am ready to go. I have been thinking about this ever since you got here, Bill. It may be a little premature from the standpoint of the Mexico War of Independence; but I don't think that is a problem, from what you have told us.

"My partners would be glad to run the store and our other operations while I am gone, so there is no concern there. I think we should start making a list of items we want to take the quantity of each. How many wagons we decide to take will be the determining factor, I suppose.

"Bill and Juan, I'll let you guys decide which route we should take. I know that from here, going the way Bill originally went up the Red River is the most direct and probably the quickest. However, it would make sense, to me, to go back through St. Louis. I have friends there in the manufacturing business that we could buy more wagons and equipment from; but we don't necessarily need to do that. So, what do you guys think?"

Aubrey jumped into the conversation and said, "You guys have not mentioned Donald and me, so I assume you think we need to get home to farm and are not interested in this project. Well, it sounds exciting to me, so I'm not intending to let you go without me. What do you think, Donald? Should we go home and cut corn or go to Santa Fe with these guys?"

Donald said in his slow drawling way, "Well, I've never been to Santa Fe; but I've always wanted to. Let's go with them, if they'll have us of course?"

Troy chuckled and said, "I'll just speak for the group and say we would love to have you."

The five of us talked the rest of the evening about the trip. We spent most of the time on what merchandise to take and how much of each to take.

It was decided that we would go as soon as possible and we would go up the Mississippi and Missouri Rivers. Juan and I felt good about the route we had taken to get to New Orleans. However, we thought the next time we go from New Orleans to Santa Fe, the Red River route might be worth a try. I thought, I would like to do that again.

Troy checked at the dock to see when the Cairo or some other steamboat was expected. They said the Cairo had left going north about four days before, so they didn't expect it back for three or four weeks. A new steamboat, the Clarendon, would have its first voyage starting in about six days.

We decided over supper, (it seemed like we always did our best thinking when food was available) that we would load up three of Troy's wagons with a variety of merchandise to take to and sell in Santa Fe. Once we got off the Clarendon in St. Louis, Troy wanted to check with his friends there, to see if they had more wagons and merchandise that we should take.

We worked the next four days getting the wagons loaded and the horses ready to go. Troy got three teams of mules from a friend named Tommy on the edge of New Orleans. We worked with the mules to see how well they pulled. There would be no problems with them. They did a good job.

Troy, Juan, and I worked at the list of items we were taking. In addition, we took several barrels of water and some hay. Except for while we were on the steamboats, the hay wouldn't be needed.

Balancing the load was important, so we tried to get some of each group of items on all three wagons. There were work shirts, pants and dresses on each wagon, along with several fancy dresses too. Troy and Juan talked about it and felt that fancy dresses might sell well in Santa Fe. Juan thought his friend Carlos would like to have some of them in his store. There was an assortment of fabric as well.

The list included several other categories. We took many

items for horses. There were harnesses with bits, hackamores, saddles, blankets, packs, frames, ropes, and more items.

Hand tools were another big category. We included knives in with the tools because they were probably the most useful thing you could have either in the wilderness or around your home or farm. Of course, as weapons knives were awfully important. For day-to-day usefulness, you just couldn't beat a good knife with an eight-inch blade.

When it came to other weapons, Troy wanted to take a variety of pistols and rifles he had in his shop. He had some friends in St. Louis that made rifles and pistols. He intended to buy some things from them or convince them to come along on our trip. But regardless of what he bought from them, he still wanted to take rifles and pistols from his store.

Troy had three different kinds of pistols and two kinds of rifles. One style of pistol was like the one that I always carried. It was a Henry 1813 that was designed for the U.S. Navy. The rifles were either made by Troy's friends in St. Louis or the Hawken Brothers that were in also in St. Louis. We were taking ammunition items such as lead balls, gun powder, and flints.

The final category of items was for general living. Some things were used mainly by people on the trail. Others were more for those in a more permanent situation. There were blankets, bedrolls, tin pans, cups, and utensils. We took mirrors, lamps, books, and a variety of wooden toys for children.

Word came that the Clarendon would leave the dock heading north the next day, so we took all our wagons and other equipment to load on the boat. Everything was loaded by that evening, except the animals. We would load them just before we left in the morning.

Juan and I bedded down by the wagons on the Clarendon just to make sure they were safe. Troy, Aubrey, and Donald said they would be there early in the morning with the horses and mules.

11 | UP THE MISSISSIPPI

We got the animals loaded at first light along with our other personal items that hadn't been loaded the day before. It was a clear morning with a light breeze and promised to be a good day for riding on a steamboat.

The Clarendon paddled away from the dock at 8:00 am. Everyone was getting used to the idea of our trip; but nobody was as excited as I was. Frances was all I could think about.

It would take us a week and a half to get to St. Louis and we really had nothing to do until we got there. Well, of course, we needed to care for the horses and mules. And we would need to keep watch over the cargo in our wagons. Our load was valuable; but it was unlikely anybody would try to steal anything while we were still on the boat. After we got off in St. Louis was when we needed to be extra careful.

Once we got to St. Louis, Troy would talk to his business friends there. He wanted to see if any of them would like to join us on our venture or if they had some goods that Troy should buy and take along to sell. We knew that getting additional wagons should be easy enough. Getting additional mules to pull them and men to drive them might be more of a challenge.

So, for now, we would relax and enjoy the trip. From what I was seeing so far, all of us would be doing what Juan and I had done on the trip down the river, standing by the railing and enjoying the view. We decided before we left, that someone would always stay with the wagons, and at night, that is where we would all bed down.

A couple of hours after the boat paddled away from the dock, I decided to walk around the Clarendon. It was somewhat bigger than the Cairo (maybe three feet wider and five feet longer); but not much different, other than that. The layout of the decks was the same. The passenger deck above had more seating and had two or three more windows on each side. The interior was painted white to make it look brighter. The Cairo had been similar. The bottom deck was partially enclosed with walls to keep the cargo dry in case of storms. The other part of the deck was open and mainly for cargo that didn't need as much protection.

There were about twice as many people on board the Clarendon than there were on the Cairo. A couple of families had come along and the rest appeared to be businessmen or men going to St. Louis for work.

I was surprised to see Mr. Jenkins on the boat. He is the one we saw arguing with Mr. Thomas on the Cairo. We obviously needed to keep an eye on him.

One of the families was the Unruhs; John, Sarah, and two small children. The family was heading to Booneville. They intended to farm there with some friends. Their home was originally eastern Pennsylvania. Land there was expensive; because the area had been settled for a long time. The Unruhs thought moving to Missouri would provide an opportunity to start a larger farm.

The Paulsen family was headed to St. Louis to start a saddlery business with a friend that was already living in the area. Paul and Joyce Paulsen were from Virginia. They had three children, who appeared to be a few years older than the Unruh children.

Two of the men on board looked like they were going to St. Louis for office work, since their clothes were new and of a modern style. The other men looked like they would be looking for rougher work.

I planned to spend most of the first day on board with the wagons and animals. That would let my three brothers and Juan spend the day at the railing looking at the countryside. I figured that Juan and Troy could talk about old times when the two of them sailed together on the east coast.

As it turned out nobody spent much time on the rail that day. Rain was coming down all day, so everyone spent their day inside. The rain was steady; but not rough like the hard rainstorm we ran through coming south on the Cairo.

I stayed with the gear all day and didn't see anybody else there except a couple of men that came to care for their horses. I hoped that most of our days would be quiet like this one.

The rain continued for three or four more days, so we were all looking forward to some sunshine when it stopped. Finally, it did stop and the sun broke out of the clouds. After that, everybody on the boat was out on the railing enjoying the sunshine.

It was my time to keep watch again. While sitting with the gear I saw Mr. Jenkins walking around. I said, "Hi, how are you?"

He growled back, "I'll be a lot better once we get to St. Louis. I've had enough of this boat and the rain."

I asked, "Is that where you intend to stay, once we get there?"

"Not really sure," he said. "I may go farther north, but I'm just not sure. Where are you going?"

"My brothers and I are going west with three wagons of gear for some family members," I lied. I would rather him not know that we had three wagons of valuable merchandise, that was being taken to Santa Fe to sell. I didn't want him or anybody else to know our plan yet. As far as I was concerned, the longer we could keep anybody from knowing our real plan, the better it would be.

I told our whole group about the conversation with Mr. Jenkins and the lie I told him. We all agreed to tell similar stories, if anybody else asked what we were doing. It would be best to tell everyone that we were going west and not get more specific than that.

Everyone enjoyed the scenery as we paddled up the river. The Clarendon was more powerful than the Cairo and was making good time. It was a great trip overall. There were several storms; but they weren't big enough to cause the river to run higher than it already was.

The weather was enjoyable when it wasn't raining. The scenery was spectacular most of the way to St. Louis. The variety of trees, shrubs, and grass was amazing. In addition, there were many areas where the river ran right against rocky hills or cliffs on one side of the boat, and that was always interesting to see.

Over the next six days, Mr. Jenkins was often wandering around amongst the cargo and animals. I heard several other people grumbling about it and I let our group know.

We weren't aware of Mr. Jenkins having a confrontation with anybody like he had on the Cairo. In fact, I don't think I ever saw him talking to anybody except our group. He generally just kept to himself.

12 | ST. LOUIS

Finally, we reached St. Louis and were relieved to be able to get off the boat. We hitched the mules up to the wagons and got the wagons and our riding horses off the boat as quickly as we could. We didn't want to be in anybody's way.

Several wagons and six or eight piles of cargo were sitting on the dock, so I suspected that it wouldn't be long before the Clarendon headed back to New Orleans. It was good to see that business was going well. That should assure there would be steamboats available when we needed one.

Troy had been in St. Louis several times for business, so he knew right where he wanted to go. After we got the wagons off the boat, we tied our saddle horses to the back of the wagons. There were five of us and three wagons, so nobody needed to ride their horse. I assumed we weren't going far anyway. However, Troy was leading us past the part of town that had developed near the dock. When we got to the edge of town and kept going, I began to wonder where Troy was taking us.

We were following a trail that appeared to be well used. It wound through a couple of areas of hills that were covered with ash and oaks. There was a lot of undergrowth that would have made the trees hard to walk through.

Troy finally stopped at a farmhouse a couple of miles from town. It was surrounded by a grove of oak trees. There was a large two-story house with a corral and an over-sized barn. We pulled all the wagons around behind the barn and corral. There were several large dogs barking to welcome us. By that time, there was a lady coming out of the house with a rifle in her hands.

She had a fierce look on her face and was about the say something when she saw Troy. The countenance on her face immediately changed into an almost sweet smile. She said in a loud voice, "Well, Troy Rampy, I haven't seen you in forever. How have you been and what are you doing in this part of the world? The boys will be thrilled to see you. Why don't you guys get down and come on in the house?" It wasn't really a question. We did what she said. Even though she was apparently Troy's friend, she looked like someone with whom you didn't want to argue.

Once inside, Troy introduced her. He said, "Guys, this is Jo Beth Russell. She has four sons that are friends of mine. They are all outstanding craftsmen and make a wide variety of things useful to trappers and travelers. Their shop is in town but I wanted to come out here and surprise them. And I wanted to see how Jo Beth was doing too. She is a skilled craftsman and taught the boys most of what they know."

"Now that's a bit of a stretch calling me a craftsman," she said. "But thanks anyway, Troy. I suppose I taught them some things; but they have certainly worked hard at perfecting their skills. I am really proud of them."

Troy added, "Jo Beth, I didn't introduce these ruffians with me. These three are my brothers Donald, Bill, and Aubrey. And this is our friend Juan Leos. Jo Beth said howdy to each of us and gave us each a big hug.

Troy told us how he first met some of the Russell family as Jo Beth got each of us a glass of water and started making a pot of coffee.

Troy said, "About the time I was starting my store in New Orleans, Jo Beth's oldest two sons, Jeffrey and Craig, came in the store just to see what we had for sale. They were looking for someone who would like to sell some of the things they made. I was impressed and offered to buy them supper.

After a few hours of conversation, we became good friends. They invited me up to St. Louis to see their shop and meet the rest of the family. The brothers and I have been back and forth between New Orleans and St. Louis several times in the past couple of years."

Troy added, "Jo Beth, could you possibly take us out to the barn and show us what the guys are currently working on?"

Jo Beth laughed and said, "You guys better go look for yourself, if I'm going to have five more people for supper, I'd better start cooking."

"If it's ok with you we will," Troy said.

"Help yourself, Honey. The boys wouldn't mind. They don't have any secrets from friends," Jo Beth said.

Troy led us out the back door and across the yard to a door on the back side of the barn. We opened the two large double doors, so plenty of light would get into the barn. It looked like a factory inside. Troy said the boys worked at their shop in town, but worked here too when they had time and the inclination. It seemed clear that they made weapons of many kinds, as well as a few other things. Their skill was obvious. Whatever they made was unique. We would all go to their shop, in town, tomorrow. That would certainly be a treat. The hard part would be deciding what to buy to take to Santa Fe. I'm sure Troy had an idea what he wanted to do concerning that. The three wagons we brought were as full as we wanted them to be, so if we bought more of anything, we would need additional wagons, mules, and drivers.

We spent the rest of the afternoon in the barn enjoying their craftsmanship and didn't come out until we heard several horses ride up outside.

The four riders looked cautious at first. They broke into a smile when they saw Troy. They all came over to give him a hug. Troy introduced us to the guys and they hugged us too. Our family back in Alabama was not filled with huggers, so I thought this hugging everybody might take a little getting used to. But it certainly seemed friendly. The brothers were all amazed to meet Troy's three brothers and Juan.

Troy had already told us that Jo Beth's third son was Jim and her youngest was Clint. They were both fine craftsmen like their brothers, Jeffrey and Craig. Jim spent most of his time running the shop and Clint spent a lot of his time finding other goods to sell through the shop. About half their inventory was weapons. They sold other things too. Since travelers and trappers were their main customers, they sold many things they needed such as knives, hand tools, equipment for horses, leather straps, and even some clothing.

Craig, the next to the oldest brother, finally said, "Troy Rampy, what the holy hell are you doing here, and with this rowdy looking bunch? You haven't come to rob us again, have you. I remember the last time you were here. As I recall you left with far more in firearms than we got in the way of money."

"Well, Craig," Troy said, "if you think you didn't get the fair end of the trade, why did you let me leave? I was thinking I got waylaid that time, not you." They both laughed and smiled at each other.

"What are you guys up to?" Craig asked.

"Right now," Troy said "we are snooping around your barn while your mother is making us all supper. While we eat some of your Ma's fine cooking, I'll tell you all about what we are doing."

"Sounds fair to me," Craig said.

About that time, Jo Beth yelled from the house that supper was ready, so we closed the barn and headed that way.

Over a wonderful supper of roast chicken, potatoes, carrots and cherry pie, Troy, Juan and I told the guys and their Ma what we were up to. I told them about my journey to Santa Fe and Chihuahua. Juan filled in a few spots and told them about our trip back to New Orleans. Troy told them about our current trip back to Santa Fe, to see if we can find long-term customers and maybe even suppliers there.

All of us, Jo Beth included, discussed the war of independence going on in Mexican territory and how we knew that it was soon coming to an end, or we hoped it was.

Troy told them that the three wagons we brought were full of items we hoped to sell in Santa Fe. He said we were looking for some other items to take with us. We weren't sure what we wanted to take or how many wagons we wanted all together.

Of course, they asked what we were taking so far. Troy gave them a complete rundown on what we had brought from New Orleans. For the next hour or so we all kicked around other alternatives, about what would be good to take. Everybody had good ideas. It was decided we shouldn't try to take everything. Troy suggested we should go to their store in the morning and make a final decision.

Jo Beth offered us her dining room to camp out in for the night and we did. The horses and mules were put in the corral. We got our bedrolls laid out and went to sleep.

In the morning, Jo Beth had a big breakfast of bacon, eggs, bread, and coffee. We all ate like a bunch of wolves before we headed into town to see the boys' store. We left our wagons and mules at the house and rode our saddle horses into town.

When we got into town our first stop was the dock on the Missouri to see when the next steamboat heading west might be there. There was nobody around that knew, so we needed to go back later. We headed on to the Russells' shop.

The shop was a little off the beaten path. I suppose that is why we missed it when we were here earlier looking around. The store was interesting. It was not any different than a normal shop selling weapons and other goods in the front. In the back, it was a different story.

The back was both a warehouse and a manufacturing area. Some of their manufacturing was conventional and some was not. They showed us a few of their favorite weapons which were more experimental than conventional.

Like most stores selling rifles and pistols, the Russell's had mainly flintlocks. That type of weapon used a flint to strike steel causing a spark that ignites gunpowder to propel a lead ball. They were good weapons; but were time consuming to load and a bit cumbersome to carry and use. However, they were the standard weapons of the day. With what we saw next, it appeared the standard weapon of the day might be changing soon.

New in the Russells' inventory were both rifles and pistols using paper cartridges. They were accurate and easy to load. And the cartridges were easy to carry. The Russells made their own cartridges and they were fastidious about quality and exactness. They made extra sure that their cartridges were always the same size and weight. Each cartridge carried the same amount of gun powder to propel the bullet.

Their newer pistols and rifles were certainly easy to use and effective; but people were still mainly using flintlocks and probably wouldn't want to change quickly.

They were working on new kinds of pistols. They made one that would load four cartridges at one time. The pistol had four barrels. Two barrels were side by side and the other two were under those two. To keep the weight of the pistol down they kept the barrels small. The barrels required a smaller caliber cartridge. This was a weapon they were only testing now, although they had made several of them. They thought it might be a big seller when they decided to sell them, so they had made a large supply of the appropriate sized cartridges.

Their store supplied lots of things to trappers that they might need as they headed west to the Rockies. The Russells bought the store from a man who had started it years earlier and supplied mainly trappers, as they came through going west. When they bought the store, they kept supplying things needed by trappers; but they were more interested in guns and knives.

After spending most of the morning in the store, we all went to a local hotel for lunch. There were nine of us, because the Russells closed their store for lunch and they all came along.

The hotel had a small private room that they put us in, so we could sit together. We ordered and they brought us water and coffee. We talked about what we had enjoyed seeing in their store. We talked a little about what we might buy to take to Santa Fe.

Then Jeffery Russell spoke up and said, "Craig and I have been talking about this trip to Santa Fe and think we would like to go along. What would you think if we go with you to Santa Fe? We would take a couple of wagons full of rifles, pistols, knives and other odds and ends. I talked to Jim and Clint and they would run the store while we are gone. There are a couple of friends that would go with us, as extra help and extra guns, if we run into trouble. Or if you would rather us stay out of your business, we would be glad to sell you whatever you want and we'd stay here. But your trip to Santa Fe sounds like something we would enjoy. So, what do you think?"

Troy said, "Well, frankly, I like the first option. We haven't talked much about it; but extra people on an adventure like this would always be welcome. What do you guys think?"

I said, "Sounds like a great idea to me." The other three shook their heads in agreement.

Suddenly I remembered Samuel Hawken and our previous conversation about buying some of his rifles. I said, "Oh, a thought just came to me. When Juan and I came through here several weeks ago, I talked to Samuel Hawken about buying some of his rifles. I didn't make any promises, but I still wouldn't mind buying a case or two of his rifles to take along, if it didn't bother you gents in any way. Of course, I wasn't aware of your store when we came through before. But what would you think?

Jeffrey Russell cut me off and said, "We wouldn't mind a bit. Samuel and Jacob are good friends of ours. We'd be glad to see you buy whatever you want from them. And just because we are coming along on this trip, I wouldn't want it to change any of your plans about what merchandise you want to take."

"Great," I said. "I will talk to Samuel today and see if he has a case or two that he can spare."

With that we had decided how to proceed. Now it was only a matter of timing. We would find out when the next west bound steamboat was heading up the Missouri River, with enough room for all of us and our animals and gear.

Juan and I stopped by the Hawken Brothers shop. It was closed. There was a note on the door saying that Samuel would be back soon. He was apparently running an errand or two. We waited and in about ten minutes he was back.

Samuel said, "Well, Mr. Rampy, it is nice to see you back. How are you? And, Mr. Leos, how are you as well?"

Juan said, "I am doing fine. Thanks."

I said, "All is well. How are you?"

Samuel said, "I'm doing well. Have you come back to buy a few rifles from me?

"I have," I said. "Have you got a case or two of those fine rifles of yours you would sell us?"

"That is all I have actually. Normally I wouldn't want to sell all of them; but Jacob is coming later today to bring a few cases from our other location. So, if you would like two cases, I can sell you that many today."

"Well, I would be happy to buy two cases today," I said.

"However, I'll need to bring a wagon in the morning and pick them up, if that's ok?"

"Certainly, that would be ok," he said. "I'll see you when you get here."

Juan and I said goodbye to Samuel and caught up with my brothers. I told Troy about the agreement I made with Samuel Hawken. I told him that Samuel would be expecting us to come by his shop in the morning.

Steamboat travel on the Missouri River was relatively new, so the boats were not overrun with business. That was good because it would probably leave enough room for us and all our gear and animals.

Jeffery checked with the dock for a steamboat going west on the Missouri. He found that the Janette was due in a few days. It should have enough space for all that we had. As far as anybody knew there weren't but a few people and not much cargo going on this voyage. The boat captain should be glad to have us.

The next morning Troy and I went into town and loaded the two cases of Hawken rifles in the wagon. At the Russells' house, we put one case of rifles in one of the other wagons to even out the loads.

The Russell brothers spent the next couple of days deciding what to take and getting two wagons loaded for the trip. Jeffery talked to his friends, Randolph and Terrance Elliott, who were going with us on the journey. They were ready to go.

Randolph and Terrance were also craftsmen, with a shop of their own. They had a small shop where they had done mainly custom work, especially on knives, pistols, bridles, and other intricate metal work. The Russells had been trying to talk them into merging their shops. This trip would be a good time to do that. They were taking a wagonload of their wares along with us and closing their shop, for the time being. We would have six wagons full of merchandise to take to Santa Fe. That would give us a good size group.

Both the Russells and the Elliotts had one employee each they were bringing along for extra help, so we would have six wagons and eleven men in our caravan to Santa Fe. That sounded like a substantial group. If we had any problems along the way, our group could probably handle it.

Three days later the Janette docked in St. Louis. The crew of the Janette would spend a few days on minor repairs before we steamed west.

Once we got word the Janette would leave the next day, our wagons and animals were brought to the dock and loaded that evening. Since we would be on the Janette for as much as three weeks, we arranged to have someone deliver a wagonload of hay to the dock. With all the mules and horses that we were taking, it would take a lot of food and water. Water could be gotten out of the river, but hay had to be brought along.

We didn't add anything to our load in St. Louis except for the two cases of Hawken rifles. The Russells' filled their two wagons mainly with cases of traditional rifles and pistols; but they had a couple of cases of their four-barrel pistols and the paper shells fired by the pistols. There were a couple of other cases for some weapons I was not familiar with. They took some of the items they would usually sell to trappers heading west to the big mountains. Their wagons were getting heavy, so they didn't fill them all the way to the top. They did bring some spare wagon parts in case of any mechanical problems.

The Elliotts' wagon was loaded with an assortment of things they had manufactured. There was a variety of knives. Most of them were sheath knives, but they had some folding knives, pistols, and hand tools that they had made. They were also bringing a couple of cases of bridles and other leather items.

The next morning the Janette left the dock as the sun had just come up. All eleven of us were on board, in addition to Frank Simmons that worked for the Russells and Ralph Taber that worked for the Elliotts.

We were lucky that only a small amount of additional cargo was on the Janette. Our six wagons were a load by themselves. When you added our horses and mules, it was almost too much. There were several dozen metal rings bolted into a beam that ran along the walls on each side of the boat. All the livestock were tied to the rings. We would feed and water them where they stood.

13 | WEST ON THE MISSOURI

Heading against the current on the Mississippi River was not as noticeable as heading against the current on the Missouri River. The Missouri was rougher. It was a much narrower and shallower river that channeled all the water flowing through it into a much smaller course. The Mississippi was as much as a mile wide in places, so the water flowed relatively smoothly.

We were in mid-summer, so the weather was hot. Fortunately, the Janette made its own breeze as it moved through the water and we remained comfortable most of the time. Of course, it was always better if you kept as far from the steam engine as you could.

The views we had seen along the Mississippi were intensified on the Missouri because we were much closer to the banks and vegetation on them. We could all spend hours along the deck railing watching the scenery. It was like the scenery along the Mississippi; but we were just much closer to it.

Mile after mile the Janette paddled upriver. It was an impressive piece of work. I loved being on board and was in no real hurry to finish our trip, except for Frances waiting in Chihuahua. I missed her constantly. I knew I had to get to Santa Fe with our current load first. Then I was going to Chihuahua, which was 550 miles farther.

We intended to have constant guards on our wagons and additional gear. Besides our group there was almost nobody on board; but there was a lot of cargo. The Janette's Captain, Henry Felder, seemed especially glad to have us on board and we were glad to be there too.

Jo Beth had sent a lot of food with us for this part of our trip, so most of our eating was done near the wagons. However, we did purchase some food from the kitchen on board, so they wouldn't be completely without meaningful work.

Even though the Missouri was much smaller than the Mississippi, it still carried a great deal of water. The Missouri River was pretty much bank full as we headed west. I couldn't help but wonder how that would affect Captain Felder's skills at following the river channel. I was hoping that he would not have any problems. He had been doing a good job so far.

There were places where the Missouri River was over a half mile wide; but it wasn't normally like that. In some places it would narrow down to three hundred feet. Even at that, the channel where a steamboat could travel was often barely wide enough for the boat.

After eight days of hard paddling, the Janette got to Booneville. She was to be docked there for one day while more wood and water for the boilers was brought on board. The captain hoped for some more cargo and passengers.

The next morning as the boat was getting ready to leave, two men came on board. They both looked like they might be bankers. Each man had a travel case which looked heavy and they both wore nice suits with vests.

Three additional men came on board a few minutes after the first two. The three men were all wearing pistols on their belts.

That struck me as a little odd. We didn't generally wear pistols on board; because we didn't see the need. I thought maybe our group should talk about that.

I was the only one of our men to see the new men come on board. Everyone else was back with the wagons and animals. I went down to discuss the issue of carrying guns with everyone else.

Juan and I had worn a pistol all the way from Santa Fe until we boarded our first steamboat on the Missouri River. Somehow being on a boat made life seem a little more civilized, so we didn't think we needed them. Now we would soon be heading across less civilized countryside, so maybe it was time for weapons again.

I got our group together down by the wagons and told them about the three men wearing pistols. It was decided that we should wear our pistols again, for the rest of the trip. We would have all been wearing them again soon anyway.

The Russell men had brought a couple cases of their four barreled pistols and several cases of the paper cartridges. They gave us each one to wear as our handguns. The pistols were lighter in weight than what we were used to. It would have been nice to do some target practice with them; but this was not the place to do that. Once we get off the boat in a few days we could practice with the pistols. Jeffery Russell assured us that they should shoot much like our flintlock pistols except, be lighter and faster to use.

It wasn't long until Captain Felder came to see us. He said the two men who looked like bankers were a little concerned about the men wearing pistols who followed them on the ship. He wasn't sure what they might do while they were on the boat; but the two men were concerned none the less.

Apparently the two men were bankers and had brought with them two cases loaded with bank notes. They were taking them to a new bank at the next stop. That is where Juan and I had gotten on. It would still be several days before we got there.

The two men hadn't thought it necessary to bring guards with them, since the trip was relatively short and the captain had originally told them that our group was the only one on board. But at the last minute, the other men bought passage on the Janette and boarded.

The day was going well. The scenery was varied although most of us had stayed with the wagons and didn't go up on deck much. It seemed like it would be prudent to stay with the wagons and animals most of the time. This was especially true with people on board that looked suspicious.

The Janette had been underway for probably no more than an hour when suddenly we heard the boat's steam whistle making repeated long blasts. This was to make us aware there was a problem. In addition, we could tell that the paddlewheels had stopped propelling us forward. We all came up on deck to see what was happening. Some of us were on one side of the boat and the rest were on the opposite side.

It was obvious the boat was in a narrow channel within a few yards of the edge of the river and a large tree had fallen across the channel. Apparently, the boat would not be able to go around the tree, so we had to stop and remove the tree. About that time, I saw three men on horses approaching the boat. Each one was leading another horse.

I heard yelling up forward in the passenger area. Next shots were fired. The two of us on our side of the boat moved forward to see what was happening. I'm sure the ones on the other side moved forward too.

Suddenly, we saw the three men who had been wearing the guns run out onto the deck. They had the bankers' bags.

It appeared that they were going to get off the boat and go with the men who had just ridden up. The only problem was that the boat was still too far from land for the men to jump across. The boat was now sitting still in the water.

It rubbed me the wrong way that these guys were stealing the bags of bank notes and may have shot the bankers. I pointed my pistol their way and yelled, "You can drop those bags right there, if you want off this boat today!"

The three men turned my way and one sent a lead ball whizzing my direction. I could hear the ball hit the bulkhead somewhere behind me, causing a shower of wood chips.

It seemed like the other two had the same idea. As they lifted their weapons, several other pistols barked. The man that had shot toward me fell, either dead or seriously wounded with what appeared to be two wounds in his chest. One wound was high on the right side of his chest. The other was lower on the left side.

The other two men were alert enough to duck for cover. They both fired from there; but I had moved through a doorway into the cargo area.

Donald and Aubrey moved forward to get a better view of the two men on board. The men on horseback started to fire about that time toward those of us on the boat. They had been confused at first; but tried to help their partners on the boat by firing toward anyone else they could see on the boat. They really hadn't counted on there being eleven weapons on the boat firing back at them. As they fired, most of our group returned their fire. Two of them were hit and fell off their horses. The third rider was hit too but stayed on his horse. At that point he seemed to decide it was time to leave. He rode away toward the east; but it seemed unlikely that he would get far.

As all of this was happening, Donald and Aubrey got in a position where they could see the other two men on board. They yelled at the two men to throw down their guns. The men turned to fire; but didn't get any shots off before being hit. They both staggered and fell.

Once the smoke had cleared a bit, we checked on the bankers. They had both been wounded but would be all right. The older one of the two was hit in his right arm. The other one was hit in the left leg. We needed to patch them up as well as we could and hope there was a doctor when we got to our final stop in a few days.

Miraculously none of our group was hurt, although one bullet almost parted Troy's hair, and another cut a gash in Juan's left arm near the shoulder.

The three men on the boat who had attacked the bankers were dead. One of the men on shore was dead and the other one was seriously wounded. The one that rode away might survive, if he could get to a doctor.

Nobody on the boat had any idea who these men were. We hated to bury them in unmarked graves somewhere beside the river, even though I was sure that happened often in this sparsely inhabited part of the world.

Captain Felder suggested that we turn the boat around and go back to Booneville. There was a marshal there, so we could tell him our story and give him the bodies and the wounded man to deal with.

That sounded like a reasonable idea to us, but turning the boat around was going to take some time. First, we had to manage to get the tree out of the river channel to proceed forward.

Troy had brought about ten axes to sell, so he dug two of them out of a wagon along with a strong rope. Don and I threw the rope around the tree and tied it off, so we could pull it up on shore once we hacked it loose from its trunk. The cottonwood was soft wood, so we had it cut and up on the shore in less than ten minutes. We let Troy have his gear back to load and we all got back on the Janette.

The dead man on shore and the wounded man were already loaded onto the boat. While that was being accomplished, Captain Felder got the boilers fired back up on the Janette. As soon as everyone was on board, the Janette started upriver.

About a half hour later, Captain Felder found a wide and deep part of the channel where he could turn the boat around. It was not easy but he managed to do it. I had never seen a steamboat turn around in the middle of a river. Captain Felder had simply guided the Janette over toward the north bank of the river where power of the water was much less than the main channel. All at once he turned the Janette as hard as he could toward the south bank. When the front of the boat got into the main channel, the force of the water pushed hard against the front and turned the boat around.

It looked easy when Captain Felder did it. I thought I would rather stick to driving a wagon pulled by some mules. Or better yet, I would just like to ride Morgan.

It was late in the day by the time the Janette got turned around; but there was a full moon, so the boat continued on to the east. It was midnight by the time we got to the dock at Boonville.

The marshal, a man named Peters, came to the dock and took charge of the bodies and the wounded man. He said he would get their local doctor to take care of him once he had looked after the two bankers.

The wounded man and bodies were not known to him; but he had seen them around town together over the past six weeks. He said he would keep an eye open for the other man that rode off.

Booneville had the only doctor in the area, so if the wounded man was strong enough to come into town to see the doctor, they would probably catch him. Mr. Peters said he would tell the doctor to be careful.

All our group, the captain and the bankers, told the marshal what had happened on the boat. We each signed a short written statement telling our stories. The marshal said we were free to go, so we headed to the Janette.

It was the middle of the night by the time we got back to the boat, so the Janette waited until the sun came up that morning before she left the dock.

The bankers were apparently going to be okay and would try

the trip again soon but with guards for their bank notes. They thanked us profusely for our help. They wanted to give us money but we refused it. We told them that we were glad we could help.

It was good to be headed back upriver. The Janette had lost a day from her journey; but we were all fine and that was the important part. Once the Janette got to her next dock, it would be time to get on the trail toward Santa Fe. I couldn't wait. The sooner we got on the trail, the sooner I would be able to see Frances. Once we got to Santa Fe, I would still have hundreds of miles to go to reach Chihuahua; but it would be much closer than I was at that moment.

The rest of our journey by the Janette went swiftly. We had so many things on our minds that we weren't even thinking about this trip.

When the Janette got us to the end of our steamboat journey at the Village of the Kanza, we decided to stay there a few days before heading west.

It took several hours to unload our animals and equipment. The mules were restless and difficult to handle since they hadn't gotten any exercise in weeks. I would certainly be upset if I were them. They did finally settle down as we drove them around for a while to get them ready for the trip.

14 | THE EAST END OF THE KAW RIVER

Our first stop was to see Francois Chouteau at his trading post. He was happy to see us.

"Juan and Bill, it is so good to see you," Francois said. "How have you been? How was your time in New Orleans? And who is this army you have brought with you?"

Juan and I both gave Francois a big hug and told him how glad we were to see him again. It had only been a few months; but it seemed like a long time since we had left there for New Orleans.

I made the introductions. I said, "Francois, I want to introduce you to our group. I told you Juan and I were going to New Orleans to see my brother Troy. This is Troy and these are my other brothers, Donald and Aubrey. They were visiting Troy in New Orleans when we got there. And we tricked them into coming with us on our trip to Santa Fe." Francois shook hands with all three of them with gusto.

Troy said, "Francois, I am glad to meet you. I know some of your family back in St. Louis and have heard of you. I thought we might have the chance to meet some day."

"Troy, I have heard of you too," he said.

Francois turned to the rest of our group and I continued my introductions. I said, "And these gentlemen, are Jeffery and Craig Russell and their friends Randolph and Terrance Elliott, Frank Simmons, and Ralph Taber. They are all from St. Louis. The Russell's and Elliott's are craftsmen and make some fine weapons. And gentlemen, this is Francois Chouteau, owner of this trading post. He is originally from St. Louis."

Francois, with a big smile on his face, said, "Bill, I am sure that you were unaware but I have known some of these gentlemen my entire life. What a joy that you have brought them here to see me. I assumed that one of these days, with the steamboat coming here, I would see them again."

Francois moved around the room speaking to each man. "Jeffery, it is great to see you. How is Jo Beth? Is she still working as hard as always?" And turning to Craig to shake his hand, he said, "Have you gents brought me anything new to sell?"

Craig spoke up and said, "As a matter-of-fact, Francois, we have brought you a few things that we will be showing you in a little while. It is certainly good to see you, my friend." They shook hands again and Francois continued around the room shaking each hand asking each man questions about their families.

Francois knew the Elliotts; but he hadn't known them as long as the Russells. He had a few of their pistols and hand tools in his trading post and was anxious to see what new items they had.

A lot of talking needed to be done. Standing in the middle of Francois' trading post was not the place for discussion, so we broke up our group and decided to reconvene at the hotel for supper, after Francois closed the trading post for the day. We would head to the hotel soon and see if they had enough room for all of us.

Thankfully we were all able to find a room for the night at the hotel. They were happy to have such a large group and said it would be ok if we stayed several nights. We would probably do that.

As I was checking in at the hotel, the clerk said, "Oh, I think I have something for you Mr. Rampy. Let me go check in the back room. He returned with a letter.

I said thanks to the clerk and almost fell down. It was a letter from Frances. My legs were shaking, so I found a chair and sat down. By the time I finished Frances' sweet letter, I was crying like a baby. I wanted to go saddle up Morgan and head to Chihuahua that minute. But I knew I couldn't do that now. Hopefully our trip to Santa Fe would go quickly.

My crying had drawn a crowd from our group. They were all wondering what was wrong. When I told them I had just received a letter from the most wonderful girl in the world, they all began rolling their eyes and making fun of me. But I didn't care; because I had a letter from Frances.

That evening at supper we all told our stories. I told about going from New Orleans to Santa Fe and Chihuahua and meeting Frances. I told about Juan and me going to New Orleans. Juan told his story of meeting Troy and eventually going home to Santa Fe and opening his Trading Post. Troy told his story about sailing, meeting Juan and settling down in New Orleans. Aubrey and Don told their stories. And finally, Francois and the rest told their stories.

Our storytelling took the whole evening and we all had a great time. Francois was about ready to go with us to Santa Fe but we worked hard to get him to stay where he was. After all, someone needed to stay in place and furnish the goods people need for their travel and lives.

We decided we would spend a couple of days here relaxing before heading toward Santa Fe.

Those days flew by and all at once we were on the trail. It was going to be a long, hot, dusty ride to Santa Fe; but I couldn't wait. It was early June 1821.

Juan and I should have been able to retrace our steps to Santa Fe; but it was not as easy as one might think. We started to the southwest on what we thought was our original track into the Village of the Kanza. However, after a while it didn't seem quite right. We kept moving knowing that it was at least the right direction.

The countryside was filled with tall grass and large trees. There were many kinds of oaks along with ash, birch, sycamore, elm, and hackberry. And, of course, wherever there was water we found lots of large cottonwoods. It was almost like being home in Alabama, except this was much hillier than where we grew up.

Our first day was invigorating. It was really the first day of having our wagons pulled by their teams of mules. Up until now we all had it easy traveling by steamboat. Now we had about 600 miles ahead of us. It would test not only the mules, horses, and wagons, but all eleven of us. If we could keep the problems to a minimum, it should be a good trip.

We brought lots of food and water; but we were hoping to find more along the way. Indians were a concern but not overly so. They probably would not bother us, if we didn't bother them. It was nice to be in a large enough group that there at least seemed to be some security.

That first day the land was gently rolling with some hills and valleys, but nothing that caused us any effort to get across. Juan, on his horse Red, rode far enough ahead that he could see any problems before we got to them. He would let us know if we needed to change course to avoid steep rocky hills or deep water.

We found a nice area to camp in by early evening. After all this was our first day of real effort, so it would be good to take it relatively easy. The area where we stopped had a spring and a grove of pecan trees. They were as tall as I had ever seen pecans, so they must have been old. It was too early for them to have nuts; but I thought we might return through this area in the fall when they were ready to harvest.

Juan decided he would try his snares again to see if he could catch some squirrels. He hadn't tried any snares since we had left this area on the way east. This spot wasn't exactly where we had stopped before but it had to be close.

Around our evening campfire everyone shared their thoughts of the day. In general, we thought it had been a good day.

As we were settling in around the fire, I said, "Juan and I wanted to find the same path we used on the way east but I think we missed it. I know we are in the same area, so we can't be too far off the path. Obviously, we need to keep going the right direction and find a path that the wagons can make good time on. Juan and I had been thinking about that for most of our trip east. It was clear that we would be coming back in wagons instead of by horse back. "

"Bill, I'm not sure we aren't on the right path," Juan said. "I think it just looks different since it was two months ago that we were here. If it isn't the right path, it is close. I'll get out early in the morning and do some scouting to find us a nice smooth path."

Jeffery said, "Craig and I have been happy with our wagons. They rode smoothly and were easy for the mules to pull."

"We are happy with our wagons also," Troy said. "Of course, what really matters, is will they last the miles it will take to get to Santa Fe. I know that we all have brought some heavy grease for the wheels and spare parts, so hopefully the wagons will do well."

Juan said, "Bill, since we are talking about breakdowns, why don't you tell everybody about our breakdown on the way to Chihuahua. I know that it is difficult for you to tell the story, but I think they would like to hear it. And if you get too emotional, I'll finish up for you."

I was a little reluctant to tell the story but agreed that I should tell it. So, after a minute of collecting myself, I said, "Well, I'll do my best to tell it. Juan is right, this story is difficult for me to tell. And I know that some of you have heard parts or all of it before. I'll try to give the short version, so I will get finished before the campfire goes out. It all started with a broken wagon on the trip to Chihuahua. Our group was large. There were fifteen wagons and thirty men, so we felt generally safe from attack by Indians or bandits. The one thing we forgot was that we were safe when we were all together. One day around noon, there was a wagon that needed repairs, so that wagon stayed behind the main body of the group after a noon time break. Repairs would be made and then the wagon would quickly catch up. Or at least that is what we all thought. There were three wagons that stayed behind and five men. The broken wagon had a driver and co-driver. And the wagon driven by the person that was going to repair the wagon and his co-driver. I stayed behind in the wagon I was driving just in case there was a problem. Juan, who was my co-driver, was on his horse Red, out scouting for problems. Well, there was a problem and we didn't have enough men to take care of it. Just as the wagon was repaired and we were about to go rejoin the main caravan, we were suddenly attacked by ten Apache braves. It happened so suddenly that we could not respond quickly enough. The braves shot a couple of arrows each before we got our first shots off. Some of the first arrows hit the two men on the repaired wagon." I started to choke-up; but caught myself and continued. "They were both killed. We managed to get some shots off at the braves and most of them were either killed or seriously injured. I was hit in the chest with an arrow. The arrow travelled along my ribs inside the skin and finally stopped in some of the muscle low on my side. I could have easily died from infection; but we had a man with us that had been a medical person in the Spanish Army. He saved me." I started to choke-up again and Juan told the rest of the story.

"I was out scouting when the attack started," Juan said. "I heard the commotion and rushed toward to noise. By the time I got there, the remaining Indians were riding off in a hurry. The caravan was still close enough to hear us firing our weapons. Some of the men came back to help. They got to the fight just as I was getting there and the Indians were leaving. I assumed the Indians would come back later to pick up their dead and wounded. We didn't bother with them.

"Jose and Alejandro were dead and Bill was unconscious with an arrow in his chest. We loaded them up and drove to catch up with the caravan. Jose and Alejandro were from Albuquerque, so a team of five men took their bodies back there to their families.

"Carlos Poso, one of the men in our group, took the arrow out of Bill's chest and doctored him for weeks on the trail. Like Bill said, Carlos did have a great deal of medical experience from his time in the Spanish Army."

I jumped into the conversation to add, "I was extremely lucky that the arrow had only sliced through my skin and hadn't hit too much muscle or bone. I was lucky that we had Carlos along on the caravan. I probably would have died without him. You can't get any luckier than that. We all felt devastated about Jose and Alejandro's deaths. It was overwhelming at first. But we all knew that something like that attack could happen when we decided to go on the trip."

We knew that our situations were not that much different now. This group was even smaller than the group that went to Chihuahua. We were in territory that was not overly familiar to us and we didn't know much about the Indian tribes in the area we would be crossing. The only difference was, that as far as we knew, the Indians in this area were not openly hostile to anyone. Obviously, we all hoped it would stay that way.

The night passed quickly and then the smell of coffee over a campfire woke me. Troy had brought a large pot for coffee, so he made enough for everyone to have a cup.

Juan had been successful with his snare and got a squirrel in each of his four snares. We all shared a little though it wasn't enough for a meal. All of us appreciated Juan's skill with a snare. Snares were a good idea. From now on we might all try to develop some skill in that method of catching small game.

The day was again clear and calm as we headed west. It was going to take a while to get to Santa Fe; but we were hoping the weather would be decent for at least most of the trip.

Juan headed out early to start his scouting. He was riding ahead of us a half mile or so looking for the best route. He managed to find us a smooth route with little in the way of difficulty. Ahead of us was the area where we knew there were miles of tall rocky hills. We weren't looking forward to that. The hills were striking and had lots of tall grass, some of it as tall as our horses. But there were many places where the hills were too steep to ride up on a horse and pulling a wagon would have been impossible. Hopefully Juan would find the trail we took the last time. It had been a relatively smooth and flat. I wasn't so much concerned about having smooth ground as I was about not having a path too steep or rocky to follow. We, no doubt, could find our way around any problem; but it would take more time.

The trail that Juan picked was just right for us and the wagons. I was pretty sure it was the trail we were on the last time.

At the campfire that evening everyone was excited about the day. It had been a relatively easy day for traveling. The path had been smooth and the weather had been pleasantly warm with just a light breeze. I told them that the next three or four days would be some of the hardest; because of the tall rocky hills we would be crossing.

Juan said, "Bill is right about the next few days being hard; but you will find it attractive, with tall grass covering hills and many rocky areas. You will certainly think that you can see the hand of God at work in those hills. And if I can find us the right trail, it might not be as hard as it would be otherwise. I will do my best to keep us away from too many problems."

Donald spoke up and said, "I don't really care how steep it

is. I just want it to be smooth. My backside is already so sore I can just barely sit down. I may have to saddle up my horse tomorrow and ride up front with you, Juan."

We all laughed at Donald's comments as he rubbed his seat. But most of us were feeling the same way. It seemed to me that every long trip on a wagon started with a breaking-in period for all our body parts, particularly the backside.

The next morning, we hadn't gone far before we could see the tall hills in front of us. They were striking; but looked a bit intimidating. Juan had taken off early to find us a good path. He was back already and thought he had found the trail he and I had been lucky enough to find going east.

We followed Juan's directions and they turned out to be just about perfect. By noon, when we stopped for a rest, everyone had good things to say both about the route and the scenery. It was especially beautiful this time of year. Most of the flowering trees were finished blooming; but there were still some with showers of white blooms. And there were some flowering shrubs that seemed to bloom for the entire summer. The trail was pretty good also. Of course, there were rough spots from time to time caused by rocky outcroppings. There also were streams that we had to cross; but most of them were dry because it had not been a rainy spring.

Juan took off again while we were resting and told us he would be back in a few hours. He wanted to make sure we were headed on the best trail by the time we got to the end of the day.

We had a good afternoon. The grass we were riding through was tall. There were several types of grass, all taller than I had ever seen. It came way up the sideboards on the wagons which were about six feet. Some of it was over the sideboards.

Late in the afternoon Juan came back and said he liked the trail we were on, so we would keep moving that direction. He thought in another day or two, we would probably be past the hills and into flatter country.

There was something up ahead that Juan wanted us to see, so we followed him. His path headed up hill until we were almost to the top. We all got off our wagons and walked to the crest of the hill. The hill was flat on top. He continued to lead us to the other side of the hill. From there we saw an Indian village that was almost unbelievable. It looked like a city. There had to be enough living space for five hundred to a thousand Indians. There may have even been enough space for twice that many.

A river, probably the Kaw, flowed from west to east on the north side of the Indian village. It looked like an ideal place to live. I wondered if this was a permanent location. I had always heard that Indians lived like nomads, moving from location to location. They had certainly put a lot of effort into this site. It would be a hard village to leave behind. The structures they lived in were domed on top and about ten to fifteen feet in diameter. It appeared the structures were topped with straw or mud. It was impossible to tell exactly what they were made of. I couldn't tell for sure, even with the telescope that I always kept in my saddlebags. Nobody in our group had ever seen a village like this one.

Their village was probably a mile north of our location, so details were hard to see. It was still unbelievable. Nobody wanted to get any closer. We were all amazed at the sight. We looked at the village for fifteen minutes or so. After our little interlude, we headed back to our wagons and proceeded west.

We were on the trail for another hour before we found a good campsite. It had been an good day. We had made the distance that we wanted to make and seen some interesting sights. I'm sure we all went to bed that night thinking of that Indian village. Wow, it was big.

As it turned out, where we camped that night was closer than we realized to the end of the hills. I'm sure that all of us were glad we had come to the end, of the lovely, but difficult to cross hills.

Our camping had been much like we had learned to camp on our trip to Chihuahua. We pulled our wagons into an oval-shaped corral at night, so that we could keep the horses and mules penned up. We also posted guards during the night. We didn't think that we would likely be attacked by Indians or bandits at night; but we wanted to be careful.

The thing that bothered me about hills was getting stuck going up an area that was too steep and having to turn around and go back down or going over some area that was too rocky and damaging a wagon. But we were lucky and got through the area without either of those problems. It had been a successful crossing of the hills.

That next morning over our coffee and breakfast, I explained to everyone that our next objective was to find the bend of the Arkansas River. I told them that it was still a couple of days away. I said it shouldn't be difficult to find. If we are going too far to the south, we would run into it and have to go north before we took it west. And if we are too far north, we would likely run into the marshy area where we killed some geese when we came that way before.

I thought finding the marshy area might be a good idea. If we could gather some ducks or geese for a meal or two, everyone would enjoy that. However, if we ran into the river before the marsh, I wouldn't go too far out of my way for a goose.

Our camp that night was in a grove near a small lake. The lake must have been fed by a spring because the water was cold.

Around the campfire that evening, Clint Russell said it appeared there were getting to be fewer trees as we went farther west. He wondered if that was the case.

I told everyone that when we started on the Arkansas River out west, the grass was short and continued to be short for several hundred miles. There were only trees up close to the river or streams running into it. I said that after that, the grass eventually changed over to taller varieties and there started to be more trees. I told them that from where we were currently, the tall grass would gradually change and in a hundred miles or so there would be a different variety of grass that grew much shorter. I told them how we had seen huge herds of bison living on this short grass, so it must be good food for wildlife.

The next morning, we started off thinking that the Arkansas River was the objective for the day, although we might not find it until the next day. It was a good day for traveling. The land was flat and smooth with just enough breeze to keep the afternoon heat bearable.

Juan was out front all day and came back later in the day. He said he had seen what he thought was the marshy area on the horizon. He could identify it from a distance; because a cloud of birds was flying in the air above it. We decided to stop by there tomorrow for a hunt and try to get on to the river before nightfall.

Before we got to the marshy area, we found a good campsite. It was comfortable with shade and water and plenty of room.

The next morning, the Russell's pulled out some weapons I had heard of but not seen. They were like a modern fowling piece. Jeffrey called them shotguns and they had their own kind of shell that the Russell's had made. The shotguns were especially made for shooting birds. Tiny balls of lead were loaded into the shells, so when you fired, a small cloud of lead flew toward the bird. It almost sounded unfair; but I was willing to try it. Birds were hard to hit, especially if they were in the air. This kind of gun might improve the odds of hitting the goose of one's choice.

It took us about an hour to get to the marshes. Where we stopped the wagons, our group broke up into threes or fours. Each group took a shotgun and some shells. The shotguns would be shared, so that everyone could get a few good shots.

As the groups headed toward the birds, there began to be loud reports, so hopefully somebody was having success. Troy and I went with Jeffery and we were able to get six birds between the three of us.

Our hunting groups came back with more birds than we probably could eat; but that evening we would all do our best to eat our share. The group had shot several geese; but most of the birds were ducks. We ate a few for lunch before we got back on the trail.

That evening we did make it to the river and camped in a familiar area. We cooked all of the birds over a large campfire. What we didn't eat for that meal, we would eat the next day. Everyone had a good time sitting around the campfire eating the birds and talking about the hunt. We were all pleased with the Russells' shotguns. It had even been fun to clean the birds as we talked about the hunt, before our evening meal.

In the morning, after eating the remaining birds, our caravan headed down the north side of the Arkansas River heading southwest. Eventually the river would turn back to the northwest; but that wouldn't be for at least four or five days.

On our trip east, we had taken a shortcut to save some time. I didn't think we should do that this time. Before, we had only horses; but now we also had wagons. I was convinced that traveling near the river would be smoother and would provide plenty of water and game. We would need to cross the river at some point. I felt like the south side worked well for us before and would probably do so again. Even though we had wagons pulled by mules this time, the south side of the river would be easier to travel.

By the end of the day, we got to the point where we had seen the high rocky outcropping before on our trip east. We were sure this was the same place. It was especially distinctive.

We camped that night within sight of the rocky outcropping, but close to the river. Several of the men had set out snares. That soon became unnecessary when Jeffrey shot a young buck. Supper was especially good and several more meals would be too.

There was another congenial night around the campfire. Our large group was filled with experienced outdoorsmen. With this kind of group there were few problems and any small problem that cropped up could easily be fixed by somebody. It was especially good to have the Russell brothers with us. They could fix any mechanical or gun-related problem.

I said, "Juan, why don't you tell everyone about the bison stampede that almost took our lives on our way east?"

Juan Laughed and said, "I guess it was really no laughing matter; but it was an interesting experience. I can think that now since we survived. This story happened on a shortcut that we are not taking now, so there is hopefully no chance that we could relive the experience. Bill and I were heading east across the face of a long grassy area that sloped to the south. To the north we couldn't see how far up the hill went. We were at least a half mile from where the slope came to some trees and a small creek, when a late afternoon thunderstorm came up in the north. We had been seeing those dark clouds to the north and didn't know how close they were until we started hearing thunder and seeing lots of lightning. It seemed to only take minutes before the storm was almost on top of us. The sound of the thunder went from occasional rumbling to constant rumbling and booming.

"Suddenly, a huge heard of bison came practically flying over the crest of the hill to our north. They were heading directly toward us. We were already trying to get to the trees on the east end of the slope for protection. When we saw the bison, it became apparent that it was a matter of life or death. We rode as hard as we could and began to feel there was little hope of survival. All at once, as we were nearing the trees, the bison swerved right just enough that they passed us by."

Everyone was impressed with our story and expressed the sincere desire to not relive that event with us.

I said, "Fellows, Juan and I had intended to show you the spot where all that happened; but to do that we would have to retrace our steps on a shortcut that we took on our way east. And considering the wagons we have with us, we decided it would be best to stay by the river. Besides, there really wasn't anything special about the spot where the stampede happened. The bison were on one side of a hill and we were on the other side. When a serious lightning storm came up and spooked the bison, they came running over the top of the hill and we just happened to be in their way. We did decide after that that we should always try to be aware of what is over the hill from us. Particularly, if what is over the hill is especially large and unruly." I got a few chuckles from that.

Troy said, "Well, up till now, we really haven't seen any bison. Can I assume we will be seeing some soon?"

Juan laughed and said, "Yes, Troy, I think you will be seeing some soon. I would be shocked if you aren't surprised by the size of the animals, and in some cases the size of the herds they live in."

As the sun came up the next morning, everyone was already up. The coffee was ready and it was a clear, and so far, a cool day. The air was fresh and being close to the river made it just cool enough. Nearby was a large area of cattails and a rather large spring. We refilled our water barrels there because the spring water was fresh and cold. Soon we were back on the trail. The river was still heading southwest and would continue to do so for many miles.

Everyone took the opportunity to check their wagons and animals before we headed on up the river.

Most of what we were going through was flat lowlands. To the north there was a ridge. Our trail was nice and flat and smooth as long as we stayed near the river. We continued this way for two more days. The third day the river turned to the northwest. From now on we would look for a place to cross the river. Juan and I felt like the south side of the river was usually the smoothest side when we traveled it heading east.

Later that afternoon, we found a good crossing where the river ran over a bed of gravel. It looked like a perfect place to cross. Juan crossed with Red first and thought it was as good as we would find.

We tried a wagon and it worked well. The water came only to the wagon's axels. Everyone got across safely and with no problems.

Soon we stopped for the evening camp. The place we camped was not as attractive as some of the previous places we had stopped; but it was all right. By now it was obvious that the grass was getting shorter and trees were becoming less common. The countryside was still attractive, but in a different way. It was rockier and had more hills. It was nothing like the tall rocky hills we had crossed eight or ten days back. These hills were much shorter and gradually sloped.

Up till now we had seen Indians only a few times since we started on our trail three weeks earlier. We were pleased that they were generally a half mile to two miles away from us, when we saw them. A couple of those times, we had seen what was probably a hunting party. I'm sure they saw us, but didn't see us as a threat.

Three times we had seen Indian villages from a distance. The first two villages we saw appeared to be made up of thatched dome-shaped structures. One village looked like it might have 100 or so adults and children. The other village, which I have already mentioned, was huge. It was like a town. We haven't seen anything like that since that time.

We saw another village just west and north from where we joined the Arkansas River. They had structures that were cone-shaped. Someone in our group referred to the structures as teepees. That group probably had 50 to 100 adults and children.

We discussed Indians around the campfire one evening because we knew we would be running into or seeing more Indians along the way. After considerable back and forth about them it was decided that we should avoid contact with them, if we could. But it was also decided that if we left them alone, they would probably leave us alone. That would be our philosophy from here on. However, that could change if the circumstances changed.

Next morning, our whole group got around more slowly than usual. Yesterday must have been harder on us than we thought. We had gone farther than normal. And there was the river crossing. Even at the best of times crossing a river is stressful on horseback. Crossing on a wagon is only a little more difficult, but a lot more stressful. The thought of losing a wagon always gnaws at the entire group. We were all glad that the crossing was behind us.

Our path today was smooth dirt with few rocks. On both sides of the river, it was rocky back away from the river. Up close to the river our path was mainly soil. Sandy soil was good whether it was wet or dry. Soils with more clay caused us problems when it was wet, because the texture got sticky and slippery. There were times, of course, when the river ran down through rocky areas and we had to get back away from the river for a safer path.

At one point, I could see there was an area near the hills that looked like it had snowed. Since the day was hot it was obvious this was not snow. I finally saw it closer and realized that it was a plant of some kind. Its flowers were bright white and the plants grew close enough together that from a distance it looked like snow.

I pulled one of the weeds and looked at it more closely. I broke a stem and it had a sticky sap inside. Except for the lack of red color, it reminded me of the poinsettias that Frances and her family grew around their house in Chihuahua.

The plant made me think of Frances. If all went well, I was hoping we would be to Santa Fe in a few more weeks and then I would start my trip to Chihuahua. That would take another three or four weeks. I was getting more anxious by the day to see her.

We camped that evening in a wide grassy spot not far from the river. There was enough space to pull the wagons into an oval shape. That allowed us to keep all the animals inside the oval for safety. We liked to do that when we could. Sometimes we didn't have enough space and had to make our corral in another way. After we got the animals fed and watered, they generally were put inside our makeshift corral for the night. They were tied to the wagon that they pulled during the day and not allowed to run free, since we usually bedded down in the corral.

Over the campfire, Juan and I told the fellows again about our bison stampede story. We had begun to see a few groups of bison, since we had gotten into the shorter grass country. There hadn't been any large groups yet.

Juan told everyone about some of the large groups of bison we had seen and what an impressive sight it was to see a thousand bison at one time. I told again about the afternoon rainstorm with the massive display of lightning. Juan and I both told them about the fire, started by the lightning, and how it had driven the enormous herd of bison over the hill right in our direction.

Juan and I were both more affected emotionally by the story than anybody else, since we were reliving it as we told it. When we finished it this time, I think we both decided there was no need to tell the story again.

Our timing for the story about the bison was just about perfect because the next day about noon, we came over a hill and saw a huge herd. It was larger than the ones Juan and I had seen before. All of us stopped and just watched the bison. It was an amazing sight. The ground was literally dark brown with bison for as far as one could see. Most of the animals were standing still with their heads down eating grass. Young calves were playing with each other in small groups. There were yearling males sparing with each other, trying to push each other around.

After watching the bison for a half-hour, we decided to take our normal mid-day break. We had some water and a light lunch and then moved on. It was certainly good that the bison were not in our way. They were just far enough out of our path, that we could go by them without disturbing them.

That evening we stopped near the river in a place similar to the night before. It was a wide-open place surrounded by elms on one side and cottonwoods on the other. There was no evidence of a spring but the river water was, as usual, clear and fresh.

As we were organizing our campsite, we noticed something interesting about the area. From our map, that had taken Juan and I from Santa Fe to St. Louis, we were able to identify this area of the river. It was marked as a shortcut to Santa Fe. The river at this point was unusually wide and flowed smoothly over a bed of gravel making an almost perfect crossing.

This was not the shortcut between points on the trail that we had taken going east toward St. Louis. It was actually the start of a shortcut from this point going toward Santa Fe. There was a problem with taking this route though. Notations on the map indicated there was a desert between where we were and Santa Fe. There supposedly was a spring along the way; but only one. If you missed the spring, there was no other place to get water.

After discussing the shortcut, we decided to stick with the river and its path. We all thought that a shortcut would be a good idea, if we were familiar with it. Nobody wanted to get caught in the middle of a desert without enough water.

In reality, we always carried a lot of water with us, so running out of water was unlikely, even if we missed the spring. But I had enjoyed the way we came and felt that was the safest way to return. I was certainly in a hurry to get to Santa Fe and on to Chihuahua; but the shortcut probably wouldn't save us enough time to make a big difference.

After the animals were fed, watered, and secured for the night, we made a campfire. Even though some days and nights seemed too warm for a campfire, we usually had a small one in the evening. It was nice to sit around the fire as the temperature cooled off.

The fire was also nice in the morning for coffee, before we got back on the trail. The ashes from the night before usually had a few live embers, that could be coaxed into a small fire. You just needed to stir the ashes enough to find the hot embers and add enough twigs and dried material to start a fire.

As we left in the morning, I noticed the river seemed to parallel a low ridge. That was not unusual. It seemed like we were often seeing a ridge or group of hills on the north side of the river. I guess when rivers are being formed in any kind of drainage area, they must tend to creep one way or the other until they run into an obstacle and often a ridge was that obstacle.

This particular ridge reminded me of the slope we were riding across on the day of the big thunderstorm and bison stampede. I sure wouldn't want to do that again.

It was a clear, calm day as we rode along. This part of the trail was just about right for making good time.

At one point when the trail took us across a high spot, we saw a large Indian village in the distance. Their living structures were the cone-shaped ones that were supposedly called teepees. The camp was probably a mile away from us.

We had only seen one group of Indians close to the river on either of our trips. They apparently liked to camp on a good spring that fed into a river instead of the river itself. That made sense. It would keep them farther away from travelers like us, that wanted to stay close to a constant source of water.

We were beginning to see some different animals. I realized this was close to where we had last seen elk and antelope. As it turned out, one of the marksmen in the group shot a yearling antelope for our supper. For most of our trip we had been supplied often with meat of one kind or the other. Of course, we had eaten all of our ducks and geese early in the trip. But there were several deer later, and now the antelope.

The landscape we had been going through for the past several days was rough and attractive at the same time. The grass had completely changed over to the short grass that the bison seemed to thrive on.

Camp was made early to allow time for dressing out and preparing the antelope for supper. Several men worked on that operation, so it went quickly. Some of the meat was cooked for supper and the rest was cut into thin strips and smoked all night. The next morning, it seemed to be smoked enough that it would be safe to carry and eat later.

The antelope was ideal for supper. Later we just talked about the last few days and speculated about the next part of the trip. We were obviously making good time. It seemed to Juan and me that we were well past halfway to Santa Fe. In a week or less we should be leaving the Arkansas River. Not long after that, we would be heading south through the mountains to Santa Fe.

That evening we were approaching the area where the river had split for a quarter mile or so. It had formed an island in between the two channels.

When we were just about to a spot that looked like a good place to stop for the night, we had our first real accident of the trip. And it was a bad one. Don was driving one of the wagons down a steep part of the trail when something spooked his team of mules. They jerked sideways to the right causing the wagon to tilt to the left. There was just enough pressure on the left front wheel that something broke and the front of the wagon dropped. Don was thrown off the wagon hard and was unable to catch himself. He hit the ground like a sack of feed.

I was riding in the wagon behind Don and saw the accident clearly. I jumped off the wagon and ran down to him. He was lying in an unusual position with his head to one side. There was blood on his face and he didn't move.

Troy, Aubrey, and two of the other guys ran up about that

time. Troy and I looked at each other with a shocked look on our faces. I think we both thought he was dead.

Juan came up about that time and kneeled beside him. He bent over him for about ten seconds and said, "He is alive." He felt around Don's head, shoulders, neck, and back. Then he said softly with his voice shaking, "I don't find anything that feels like it is broken. He sure has a huge lump on the side of his head. Why don't we pick him up gently and put him some place soft over in the shade of those trees? We can clean up the blood on his face and just keep him comfortable. A few prayers would help too."

Troy and I carried Don under the trees, while someone else got his bedroll out of the wagon. We laid him on the bedroll as softly as we could. Aubrey got some water and a piece of cloth to wash his face and cool his head and neck.

Everyone one quietly got the camp made for the night and took care of the animals. A couple of the guys got the wagon repaired. I couldn't think about anything but Don. I'm sure Troy and Aubrey couldn't either.

It was quiet around camp that night. Nobody knew what to say. Juan checked on Don from time to time and he was still breathing; but had not moved at all. I was afraid he would not wake up or would wake up and not be able to move. It really terrified me. I talked to Troy and Aubrey. They were scared too.

The three of us slept beside Don that night, in case he stirred and needed anything. We didn't want him to wake up and not know where he was. He was still breathing when we went to bed. The lump on his head hadn't gotten any smaller.

In the morning there was no change. He was still breathing steady. We decided to stay put for the day and work on our equipment.

One of us always stayed with Don. Everybody else spent the day working on the wagons. We had brought quite a few spare parts for the wagons and it was good we did. It would have been impossible to manufacture them out here on the prairie with no equipment.

I stayed with Don for most of the morning and Troy and Aubrey traded off in the afternoon. We tried to keep Don as comfortable as we could.

That evening we threw a blanket over Don even though none of us really felt cool. There were a few times that evening that he scared us. Don had not moved since the accident, but suddenly his muscles clinched up. Even the muscles in his face clinched up. That happened a couple times during the evening. Troy, Aubrey. and I slept by him that night like we had the night before. We didn't notice any more movement.

The next morning, we all sat around our reconstituted campfire and discussed the previous day. Everyone had gotten the work done they had intended to do. Nobody knew what they would do, if we stayed at this camp another day. But that is what we decided to do. We thought we would stay here till tomorrow at least. We would probably move on tomorrow whether or not Don had woken up.

I guess that was logical. We had to move some time, and what if Don continued like that for another week or two? I was hoping he would wake up soon. He had hit the ground mighty hard though, so if he did wake up, I was sure hoping that his brain was all right. His muscles clinched up three or four more times that day.

Some of the guys worked a little more on the wagons and other equipment. Several got on their horses and rode around to see the countryside. When they came back later in the afternoon, they said we were about three miles from an enormous herd of bison in one direction and a large Indian village in the other direction.

That evening we decided, that in the morning we should move on. Don would be laid in one of the wagons on as comfortable a bed as we could make for him. We would put as much padding as we had under his head.

The night went quickly and we got on the trail again. Don had still not moved, other than a few more of his muscle clinching episodes. We were continuing to sleep close to him at night, so we would be aware if he moved.

The group got around slowly in the morning. I think we were all still hoping that Don would wake up; but he didn't. Everything, including Don, was loaded up and we moved on by mid-morning. We moved slowly at first not wanting to bump Don around. After a while we decided his padding was supporting him well and we began to move out at our normal pace.

It was a windy day. We saw many antelopes, another herd of bison, and a group of elk. It looked like this area had had lots of rain because the grass was especially green. It wasn't any taller than normal; but it looked good. And the trees and shrubs along the river were more robust looking than we would have expected. There wasn't nearly the variety of plants as there had been a few weeks before when we were in taller grass country.

That night we decided to let Don continue to sleep in the wagon since we didn't like the idea of moving him back and forth a lot. We had quit checking his breathing as often; but we were still doing it some. I got up in the wagon and made sure he was breathing and comfortable before I got in my bedroll.

I slept fitfully that evening. I was more worried than ever about Don since he had not woken up since the accident. We didn't know what to do. I wished there was a doctor around, although I'm not sure what they could have done for Don either.

The next morning, we got up a little earlier than normal and got on the trail. I had checked Don before we left. As usual he didn't seem to have moved during the night. But his breathing was still good.

The area we were travelling through did not look familiar that morning. That seemed unusual, since I have a pretty good memory for the trails I travel on. After a little while, it dawned on me that this was probably the part of the trail we circled around to miss the Indian village. We hadn't seen any Indians for almost a week. I was glad the village was not still here or we might have stumbled right into it.

About halfway through the morning, we stopped for a break. I got in the wagon to make sure Don was padded well. I was checking around his head when suddenly he opened his eyes and said, "Bill, what are you doing?"

I just about fell over in shock. I said back to him, "I don't know, Don. What are you doing? And where do you think you are?"

He puzzled over that last question a minute. Then he finally said, "I'm not sure where I am; but it feels like one of those fancy hotels in the big city. So, where am I?"

I said, "You are in the back of a wagon on the way to Santa Fe."

He said, "Why am I in a wagon?"

I explained what had happened and told him he had been asleep for five or six days. I told him, we had all been scared to death and I was beginning to wonder if he was ever going to wake up.

He scared me again when he said, "So why are we on the way to Santa Fe?"

I was so happy to see him awake that I forgot my earlier fears about his brain being damaged. I was hoping this was just temporary.

I told him that I wanted to go tell everybody that he had woken up, so he might be having a little company.

A few at a time, everyone came over and spoke to Don. They told him they were glad to see he was better.

I was excited that he called almost everybody by their first name. His brain couldn't be too scrambled, if he remembered everybody's name.

We got him up in a sitting position and offered him a little food and some water. He ate a little bread and drank a good deal of water. I was afraid of him going back to sleep again.

"Don, how are you feeling?"

"I feel really tired and sore."

"You hit the ground pretty hard," I said. "I'm not surprised that you are sore. A few times while you were asleep your muscles clinched up for some reason or the other. That may have made you sore too."

"I'm sure glad I didn't break my neck."

"Me too, brother, me too."

An hour or so after Don woke up, we continued our way. All of us felt greatly relieved. We would continue at a slower than normal pace for a while and probably stop a little early for the day. I thought it would be good for Don to have some time to walk around, if he felt like it.

We saw several small herds of elk close to the river. They must usually stay close to the river in this area, since that is where the taller grass grows. The area out away from the river is usually only short grass.

Our campsite that evening was near a spring-fed pond close to the river. The overflow from the pond flowed down toward the river.

Troy, Don, Aubrey, and I all walked around for a while once we got the animals settled down for the evening.

None of us knew what to say to Don. I know we wanted to tell him how glad we were that he finally woke up and how afraid we were that he wouldn't. We walked along the river for thirty minutes or so.

Finally, Aubrey said, "Don, I am so glad you finally woke up. I was scared to death you would just die. I have never seen anybody hit the ground that hard and survive. If I lost you, who would I farm with when I get back home? I know that God was looking out for you and ultimately looking out for me." He started to say something else, but was choking up and finally stopped.

"Don, I felt the same way," said Troy. "I was scared to death you would just leave us."

"Me too," I said.

We walked on down the river. It was a stunning evening and just starting to get twilight. All along the bank of the river were cattails and other tall reeds. We heard enough bullfrogs croaking that we thought about stopping to see if we could gig one or two with a sharp stick; but we didn't.

We would have gone farther; but suddenly, we heard several wolves start howling. The sound couldn't have been coming from much farther away than 500 yards. It was likely they were after one of the elk we had seen earlier. We certainly didn't want to get mixed up in their supper plans, so we headed back to camp.

The howling stopped after a while. The wolves must have gotten their elk. The rest of the night was quiet, except for a few bullfrogs croaking and lots of field crickets making the rasping noise that they make.

The next morning, we got everything ready to go and headed west. It was hilly in places; but basically, the route was flat and dry. All along the way for the past ten days or so, trees had become fewer and fewer. Now they were getting almost non-existent. There would be one or two only on rare occasions. There were still lots of reeds and cattails up close to the river, and a few cottonwoods; but they were back away from the river.

There had been numerous antelope scattered across the prairie. Mostly they were in small groups of three to eight. We did see one group that had thirty to fifty animals. We tried not to disturb them; but once or twice we did and were amazed at how fast they could run.

That afternoon we did find a little shade along the river where a grove of cottonwoods had sprung up years before and were now thirty feet tall. It was decided, that we would take the rest of the day off and do some maintenance on the wagons and other gear. We thought too, that it would be good to rest the animals. The horses and mules had done a great job for us and we didn't want to press our luck.

It was a productive afternoon and evening. Most of the little problems we had been having with the wagons had been repaired. Most issues were caused by a lack of grease. Even though we put on new grease often, it really wasn't often enough. We were always sensitive about the seats on our wagons. They just seemed to ride rough. I suppose that someday people will be putting padding on the seats, which really wouldn't be a bad idea. We didn't have any way to correct that situation except sitting on our bedrolls. Frankly, that did work well for me either.

At any rate all the wagons were back in good shape. The animals seemed to like their afternoon off too. We spent some time brushing them and letting them soak their feet in the river. They all seemed far fresher than normal in the morning.

15 | SOUTH TO SANTA FE

Juan and I had discussed our route that morning over our usual cup of coffee. Juan was thinking that we might get to the Purgatoire River that afternoon or the next morning. I told him I was thinking that we might reach it the next afternoon. Juan was right. We got to where the Purgatoire dumped into the Arkansas River about mid-morning the next day.

I was glad that we were on the south side of the Arkansas River when we reached the junction of the two rivers. It made our turn south along the east side of the new river easy.

It was interesting how small the river looked; after riding along the Arkansas for weeks. I was thinking that we spent about two and a half days on the Purgatoire on our trip from Santa Fe, so it wouldn't be long before we got to the mountains.

Over the next couple of days, we all enjoyed the ride to the south; but I for one was having a hard time thinking about anything other than getting to Santa Fe and on to Chihuahua and Frances. You would think that after a trip to St. Louis and New Orleans and back again to here, I would have my heart a little more in control. But it wasn't working like that. It seemed to me, the closer I got back to Santa Fe, the more I thought of Frances. And this was even with intentionally trying to think about other things, such as my brothers and our childhood back in Alabama or the idea of going to law school back in the eastern United States somewhere. Law school is probably a dream that is gone for good.

I figured I would spend a week in Santa Fe as Juan and I introduced the rest of our group to all the merchants we knew. And of course, Juan and I would want to socialize with friends and family. But as soon as I could after that, I would leave for Chihuahua. I wasn't sure what Troy, Aubrey, and Don would do at that point. They might go with me to Chihuahua. Or they might head straight back to New Orleans, once they had sold their goods.

The countryside was lovely as we got more into forested areas and the end of our ride along the Purgatoire River. We could feel the elevation changing as we got into the mountains. It seemed like a long time since Juan and I had passed through this area. Even though it was only a matter of months, it felt like much longer. It made me excited to think, we were getting closer to Santa Fe by the day.

The evening after we left the river, we camped in an open area surrounded by pine trees. The smell of the pines was strong. It was a wonderful place to spend time.

Over supper I asked the entire group, if they had ever been in an area like this. Only Juan answered in the affirmative. I told them that this was how it smelled when I first went over Glorieta Pass on my way to Santa Fe. I remember loving the resinous, earthy smell then and I certainly loved it now.

Aubrey asked if Glorieta Pass was where we were headed tomorrow. I told them that tomorrow, we would hopefully get to Raton Pass. After Raton Pass, we would spend several days going through a relatively clear area for a couple of days, paralleling an area of mountains. Next, we would spend a day or two going up into the Sangre de Cristo Mountains and over Glorieta Pass. Finally, we would reach Santa Fe.

It was breathtaking on top of Raton Pass the next day. You could see for miles. The entire group got down off their wagons and stood together just staring off into the distance. It was an amazing sight. Those that had never seen a sight like this were enthralled. And that was everybody, except Juan and me.

We made it down the south side of the pass before we stopped for the night. We camped in an area that was mainly aspens and cottonwoods. I told the group that the aspens would soon be turning a striking shade of bright yellow, so they should stay in this area long enough to see that, before going back to the U.S.

The next morning, we were all having such a good time enjoying the campfire and the scenery that we didn't want to leave. Eventually we did and were soon out of the mountains into easier but less scenic travel.

By the time we had traveled another two days, we were almost where we would go up into the Sangre de Cristo Mountains. Our camp that night was in another striking area with cottonwoods on one side and aspens on the other. It was a great place to camp. The quiet really made for good sleeping too; but that didn't keep us in the bedrolls. By first light we were all up. The end of our trip was so close that everybody was restless. We just wanted to get there.

Today we would make it over Glorieta Pass. And a day after that we would be at Santa Fe.

Juan and I were rode side by side for a while. He turned to me and said, "Bill, are you getting excited?"

"Juan," I said, "you cannot imagine how excited I am. I can barely believe we are so close to Santa Fe."

"How about you, Juan," I asked? "How excited are you to get back to Santa Fe? And have you decided what to do about your trading post?"

Juan thought about it a minute and said, "I am excited to get back to Santa Fe to see my family and friends." He hesitated a minute and said, "I'm not entirely sure about the trading post. I know I want to do something, but I'm not sure exactly what."

When we got to the top of Glorieta Pass, everyone got down off the wagons and stared as a group off into the distance just like they had on Raton Pass. The view here was even more stunning than the sight off Raton Pass. The expanse was amazing. There were trees as far as you could see. It was certainly something special. I was glad to have brought this group of flatlanders to these beautiful mountains, so they could see something spectacular.

When we camped that night, we were near Santa Fe. We decided it was going to be too dark to get there safely. In the morning, we would get up early, clean up a bit more than normal and get our animals and equipment ready to go. It would be an easy ride into Santa Fe.

The next morning, we did just what we planned the night before. By about midmorning we were approaching Santa Fe from the south. Everything seemed to be unusually quiet. We didn't see anybody on the road or even any children playing in their front yards.

It became clear where everybody was, as we got near the square. There had to be something going on at the cathedral. It seemed like everybody in town was in the square for some kind of celebration.

The square was the central gathering spot in town. It was a large open area with the Governor's Palace on the west and the cathedral on the north. There were businesses on the other two sides. Almost everything of importance in Santa Fe happened on or around the square.

The Governor's Palace was an adobe building with large beams here and there for support. This was especially true along the roof of the building, which was flat. The cathedral was a much taller and more graceful looking building. It was thrilling on the inside, with ornamentation that would almost take your breath away.

We pulled up short before we got to the square. Juan said, "There must be something big going on at the cathedral, so let's make a plan for as soon as our fellow businessmen are available. When the crowd around the square gets smaller, I would suggest pulling the wagons along the side of the square. We'll leave them there and go as a group to see all of our friends that are in business. Later they can come over to the wagons or we can pull individual wagons nearer their stores. We'll spend the rest of the day seeing people. I'll leave you all with Bill for a while and go see my family. My mother will probably want to cook supper for all of us at her house. I suppose some of you will want to stay at the hotel, if they have room. The rest of you can stay at my parent's house."

Troy asked me, "Bill, what do you intend to do now that we have reached Santa Fe?"

I said, "Oh, I will stay here for a few days to see how things go with all of you. Then, I will head to Chihuahua as fast as I can go. What do you intend to do?"

"I'm not sure," Troy said. "I suppose we could stay here a while or maybe go to Albuquerque. Or we might follow you to Chihuahua. Just in case there is a wedding to attend. I guess I'll see what the rest of the gang here intends to do."

Juan said, "Let's all head over to the square. I can introduce all of you to my friends and family. Most of them must be there."

That sounded like a good idea to us. The wagons were tied where they were and we walked to the square. Almost immediately we started running into men who had gone on the caravan to Chihuahua. First, there was Sid and Carlos. Next, we saw Juan's cousin Leon the wagon maker.

Leon saw us first and yelled at Juan and me. He said, "What are you guys doing here?"

Juan said, "We just got here. What is going on in the cathedral?"

Leon said, "They're installing a new priest. It's our…"

That's as far as he got and stopped. He told Juan he needed to see him for a minute about some family business. They both walked about fifty feet to one side. After talking a minute or two, they came back laughing.

Juan said, "Let's all go over to the cathedral and see the attendees come out to the square for the celebration, that was prepared in the honor of the new priest."

Our whole group moved over that way. Most people were waiting across the road in the square, so there was room up near and to the side of the cathedral doors.

We waited there only a few minutes until the doors were both opened. First there were two priests that came slowly out. I recognized both. The new priest came out next. I was shocked. It was Ronaldo Leos. Following Ronaldo was Juan's Aunt Anita and Uncle Claudio. My heart skipped a beat or maybe it just stopped. Following Anita and Claudio were their two daughters Josepha and my wonderful Frances. I wanted to yell at her and run up and embrace her; but I didn't want to spoil the procession.

She was wearing an ankle-length olive-green dress with a brightly colored embroidered collar. Her long black hair flowed down her back. She looked absolutely stunning. Looking at her made me feel weak in the knees.

One of the family members out in the crowd that had seen me, caught her eye and pointed my way. When she saw me, she ran to me and I ran to her. We embraced and kissed like we hadn't seen each other in years, and frankly it almost felt like it.

She said, "Bill, when did you arrive in Santa Fe? I'm so glad to see you. I thought I might not see you for a few more months. When we heard that Ronaldo was coming to Santa Fe, we knew we had to come. I've been praying that you would make it back, before we had to leave for Chihuahua. Oh, Bill, I am so glad to have you back." She squeezed me and kissed me again.

I told her that it was a complete shock to see her there. I said we had no idea what was going on at the cathedral as we rode into town. I told her again how much I loved her and how wonderful it was to see her. She told me the same thing. We stood quivering as we held each other.

After we both calmed down a little, I introduced her to my brothers and the other men that came with us. We went over and talked to her sister Josepha and her parents. All three of them were both laughing and crying to see the two of us back together.

At that same time, Ronaldo saw us and came over to shake my hand and hug his sisters and parents again. He turned to Frances and me and said, "You know, this would be a great day for my first wedding ceremony. And just look at the crowd."

He said it playfully, but part of him was especially serious. Frances and I looked at each other and smiled. Then, we looked at each other again with questioning looks on our faces and both of us shook our heads in agreement.

EPILOGUE

Love between Bill and Frances brought them safely back together. They were married on the very same day in front of many of their family and friends. Father Ronaldo Leos, Frances' older brother was the officiant at the wedding. He could barely perform the ceremony, because of the tears in his eyes. He had Bill and Frances promise to be true to each other in good times and in bad, in sickness and in health. They also promised to love and honor each other all the days of their lives.

The ceremony was followed by a meal and dance. The meal was really because of the installation of the new priest; but Ronaldo was certainly willing to share with his little sister. And after all, the same group attended both ceremonies.

During the meal, Bill introduced his brothers, the Russell's, the Elliott's, Frank Simmons and Ralph Taber to all his new family in Santa Fe and Chihuahua and the businesspeople that he knew. They all had a good time making new friends.

Bill and Frances had a wonderful; but exhausting time talking to every friend and family member that was at the wedding.

The dance for Bill and Frances was an exciting family and friends gathering with almost everybody in town attending. The music and dancing stopped by midnight; but the talking and laughter lasted much longer.

A week went by in a heartbeat for the young couple and then they were off to Chihuahua with the family.

The trip was quicker than normal and safe. Claudio and Bill would soon have a second house built at the rancho. Bill, at first, would work with Claudio in the store. Frances intended to continue teaching at the cathedral. They both loved their new lives together; but as with life in general, things would change too quickly.

Within a few days after the wedding, Troy and the other men had sold all their merchandise and were thinking about their next steps.

Troy, Aubrey and Don decided to follow Bill and the Leos family as far as Albuquerque. They enjoyed their time there and spent two weeks getting to know the retail business in the area. Their intent was to go home to New Orleans to check on the store. Then they would return to Albuquerque to start a new store. Aubrey and Don would probably run that store and Troy would return to New Orleans.

The Russell's and Elliott's headed back to St. Louis with their employees. They would return to Santa Fe; but it would probably be a while before that happened. In the meantime, they would be busy making rifles and other merchandise to supply clients and bring back on their next trip to Santa Fe.

The End

Continue the Rampy Family series
Book 3: TRAIL to HOME

Made in the USA
Columbia, SC
10 June 2025

59223009R00107